WORTHY

Book One
Worth Fighting For Series

Kelly Hagen

Published by TreasureLine Publishing

www.TreasureLinePublishing.weebly.com

Cover design by Michele Barrow-Belisle

CHAPTER ONE

Three gruesome figures inched their way through the fading orange sky over the small rural town of Green Hill, Kentucky. Their mission not too far off in the distance.

Dark, leathery wings folded up behind them as they quietly landed in the top of one of the tall oak trees that surrounded their destination. They peered through the roof of the small wooden structure that had been standing for what easily looked like a hundred years. Specks of brown peeked out through the chipped white paint that covered the house. The roof above the porch was sagging in the middle from the rotten wood that had not been replaced since the house had been built. The only gutter was held on by two screws, one at each end of the house. The only real color was the small red rose bushes that lined the front of the house under the dining room window.

A long menacing cackle exited from between Latar's rows of jagged teeth. He was the largest demon of the three, standing a foot over his companions, Melti and Ackmen. Large, red, circular eyes, sat just above a very human-like nose. Raven colored skin clung to the defined muscles beneath it, leaving no question to the demon's strength. He tilted his head to the side. A grin threatened to overtake his thin lips as he watched the small lizard-like spirits of Strife,

Confusion, and Pride tear apart the family inside.

"There's no more time to waste. I want her on our side. We need her on our side," Latar hissed. A putrid green mist mingled with his words and swirled out in front of them with the motion of the wind.

"We will visit Cara tonight," responded Melti.

Ackmen's thin top lip snarled up and he shook his head in agreement. "Yes, tonight," he said as he curled his long, dark appendages in an eerie manner.

Melti honed in on the girl sitting at the table as she listened to another one of her parents' arguments. Her once vibrant green eyes that held true peace, true happiness, were now dull, tired and full of worry. Clouded by the pain within her.

"Her family has always been easy for us to control and manipulate. Do you think she'll cause any delays with her stubborn pride?" Melti questioned his superior.

"No. Her stubbornness and pride, are just what we need to work with," Latar answered. "Come, we must go."

❖ ◆ ◆ ❖

Katelyn fought against the tears that demanded to be released, and let her mind wander from her unpleasant situation to that of her boyfriend – Trevor. Even though her heart ached when she thought of the bond the Holcomb's had with one another, it was something else, anything else to help escape what was in front of her.

What holds them together? She had asked herself that question many times, and never came up with a suitable answer. Sure, there was the belief in their unseen God, but that couldn't be it. God wasn't real anyway, the best she could figure. Yet, real or not, she couldn't argue the fact that Trevor's family had an abundance of what her family seemed to lack – love.

What she had with Trevor gave her some hope, though she wasn't sure she could ever let him completely in her heart. Show him who she really was inside. Did anybody? Besides, rejection was not her friend. She'd had enough of that from the two people that stood in front of her, with their voices raised and arms flapping through the air. Each one failing miserably at trying to get their point across.

Trevor wasn't like the guys she dated before, and she had dated a lot. That wasn't something she was proud of, but the truth nonetheless. So much of herself compromised, lost, given away for the brief moments of freedom from a messed up home life. She wondered if it was worth it. If her sanity had been worth it. If *she* had been worth it.

"Mom, Dad," Katelyn took the rare moment of silence to question her parents, "Why do we have to go through this same song and dance every night? You both act like I'm not even in the same room with you. Like I can't hear what you're saying. Do my feelings matter to you? Does my opinion matter?"

Her parents' silence only added to her frustration. "I guess not. You know, I thought once I got older we'd be able to work out this whole issue concerning Aunt Cara. I figured wrong I guess." She sighed.

As far back as Katelyn could remember her mother never got along with her aunt. The reason why still kept itself hidden behind close mouths and deadly stares from all those involved. She shook her head. Cara was such a lighthearted person. So much so, that sometimes her bubbly, carefree nature passed right through the walls of those around her bringing life to what was moments before a closed off and guarded heart.

"Katelyn, honey, I just have this to say. If you knew who Cara was on the inside, you wouldn't like her. If you could see what she's hiding from you, you'd run away. Please, please listen to me Katelyn."

Her mother's pleas touched her at her core, but not enough to sever the ties that had grown so strong between her and her aunt.

Katelyn's father interrupted, "Keep quiet, Leah. Now is not the time," he demanded.

"I've kept quiet, Brice. For too many years, I've kept your family's secrets. Do you really want to see your only daughter go down the same path as your grandmother, your mother – your sister?"

Katelyn sighed. "I can see I'm not getting anywhere with either of you. I haven't for all these years, so I'm not surprised that I'm not now."

Her mother cupped her face in her hands, then kissed her on the forehead. "Your father and I have been talking about this day for a while now. I've chosen to move out, Katelyn. I can't live like this anymore. I'm asking you to forget Cara and come with me."

Katelyn stepped back under the weight of her mother's words. She sought out some type of understanding in her father's eyes, but they were cold, hard – empty.

"You can't be serious?"

"I am."

"You know what, we all need to calm down. Sleep on things. Start over in the morning."

"There will be no starting over this time, Katelyn. But I see you've made your choice. I'll be in touch soon." Leah grabbed her suitcase and nodded towards her husband, "Goodbye, Brice."

Katelyn went to call out but her tongue betrayed her. Her lips defied her.

The unseen gray spirit of rejection, small as it was, still held a mighty force of power in his webbed-like hands. It whispered of past hurts as it encircled the black haired girl standing in the middle of the room. An anger from deep within began to surface. An anger that was rooted in rejection. The rejection of a mother's love. The rejection of a mother's concern.

She turned to leave, fighting off the heaviness that had come upon her. It made it harder and harder for her to turn away from her father and towards her room.

"Katelyn wait." The warmth of her father's calloused fingers gently wrapped around her arm only fueled her irritation.

"Wait, wait for what, Dad? Mom's gone. She just walked out that door, and you...you didn't even bother to try and stop her."

She turned and without looking back pulled her arm from his grasp and let it aimlessly fall to her side.

Chapter Two

The atmosphere in Cara's bedroom changed abruptly pulling her from a blissfully sound sleep. A heaviness pressed against her chest while a tight clasp fought to cut off her airway. She grabbed her neck and sat up gasping for what ever amount of air her lungs could take in.

She glanced over at the sizeable shadow that had filled the entire corner off to her left. The one that secretly housed all her books, prayers, potions and cards, behind a perfectly made tattered bookshelf, that anyone was afraid to move for fear of it falling apart. A genius idea, she'd thought.

The dark figure whispered only three words before it disappeared taking the heaviness it had brought along with it. "It is time."

She shook her head. A sly smile tugged at the corner of her lips. "Finally," she said.

This was the day Cara had long waited for. She'd planted little seeds of doubt, fear, turmoil, and the like in the heart and mind of her niece through out her life – all twenty years of it. And all right under the nose of Katelyn's over protective mother. A scornful snicker filled the silence. Why her brother decided to fill Leah in on their family business was beyond her. Love makes you blind and foolish, she'd come to realize. That was one of the many reasons why Cara wanted no part of it. Her focus had to stay on the price, on the goal – adding another generation to the Burnsten family clan.

The radio blasted one of Katelyn's favorite songs as she leaned slightly to the right and then to the left, in sync with the curve of the country road that led to Cara's two-story farm house.

Freedom. That's what she felt overtake her as the miles increased between her and her *real* life. Or so she thought. Had she'd been able to see the wispy green bug-eyed spirit, Deception, sitting beside her toying with her mind and emotions, she may have realized that freedom wasn't what she was running to; it was what she was running from.

"Ah, there's nothing like the smell of freshly cut grass." She inhaled the aroma a few more times before finally leaving it and the buzz of the mower far behind.

The road grew narrow the closer she came to reaching her aunt's drive. She let off the gas and applied the brake, slowing down the one and a half ton machine she was behind the wheel of. The trees with their mostly green leaves were starting to become peppered with little bits of yellow, signaling that fall was just around the corner, and the hottest days of summer were now upon them.

Katelyn enjoyed the cooler air though. It refreshed her. It was like old things were buried and the new was coming. Strange in a sense, as that's what most people loved about spring; with the snow melting and the flowers beginning to peek out from their somber winter dwellings. Not her though. She had to be different, had to go against the grain.

It was the one and only thing she liked about herself — sometimes.

She turned down the radio as she pulled off the road and onto her aunt's gravel drive. Cara had been on the porch waiting for her. Katelyn returned her aunt's wave and added on a large, full teeth showing, cheesy grin. Cara just shook her head. Katelyn laughed.

"Hurry up girl, I got dinner on the table and a bunch of sites and pamphlets for us to go through. It's going to be fun!" Cara yelled.

Katelyn pulled to a stop and stepped out of the car. "Be there in a sec," she called over her shoulder as she grabbed her suitcase from the back seat. Excitement coursed through her. Planning their yearly fall trip was a favorite pastime. Their safe haven for the last three years had been the warm sandy beaches of Hawaii. She had a feeling it would be the same again this year, but she was okay with that.

Katelyn followed Cara through the front door and threw her stuff on the couch before closing the door behind her and making her way to the kitchen. All the different smells of a warm Thanksgiving Day dinner assaulted her nostrils, and brought a watery coating to the inside of her mouth.

"Mmmm, something smells good in here."

"Well, thank you," Cara replied, "I made your favorite."

The small, round table was set with white plates decorated with a deep golden flower scene along the edges. Empty tall-stemmed glasses were off to the left. Matching bowls filled with rolls, green-beans and macaroni and cheese were staggered around the platter in the center filled with turkey that had already been sliced and drizzled with gravy.

"Whoa, what's the occasion?"

"You are, silly. Come on let's eat before it gets cold."

"I'm the occasion, huh? Why?" Katelyn asked as she pulled out the chair. "What did I do?"

Cara's smile warmed her heart.

"You didn't do anything. It's just I know you've had a rough go of it recently, and your mom leaving a couple nights ago surely didn't help. So I just thought we'd have a nice dinner. Ya, know? Maybe remember how things used to be when you were little and you had both parents around all the time. Speaking of parents. Have you talked with your mom?"

Ouch, Aunt Cara. That stung a bit.

"Thank you," she smiled, "I appreciate the thought, and no I haven't talked with Mom. I want to call her. I just don't know what to say, yet."

"You can't let them bring you down, Katelyn. You have your own life. You need to make your own mistakes, learn and grow. They've lived their lives, now it's your turn."

"I know, it's just, oh I don't know," she sighed in frustration.

"I don't either. I mean, you could be hanging out with someone a lot worse than me."

"True."

"So," Cara said handing a pamphlet her way, "What do you think about going here this year?"

"Hawaii?" Katelyn questioned around the food her mouth, half smiling.

"Now what's wrong with Hawaii?"

"Nothing, trust me."

"I thought that might be what you'd say."

"You know me too well, Aunt Cara."

"Yes, yes I do. So, Hawaii it is then?"

"Hawaii it is."

Katelyn stuffed the last bite of food left on her plate in her mouth, then asked, "Do you still want to meet up with the boys at the bar tonight?"

"Of course. Besides I know you can't go a day or two without seeing your man."

"Funny, Aunt Cara. Real funny."

"It may be funny, but we both know it's the truth."

Katelyn rinsed off her plate, then set it in the sink. "Hurry up then, I can't wait to let loose tonight."

"Go on and change, I'll be up in a minute."

"Okay."

Katelyn started up the steps and was overcome by a strange feeling. The hairs on the back of her neck stood on end and she couldn't help but feel that someone, or something was staring a hole right through her. She ignored it and continued to the room Cara had made up for her.

CHAPTER THREE

Katelyn threw her purse in the chair then fell back on the bed. A tired smile crossed her lips as she remembered being in Trevor's strong embrace as he swung her around the dusty dance floor. He had eased the pain. Though the hope of it being completely erased by the fruit flavored liquid had sadly fallen short. She bobbed her head gently to the rhythm from the live bands drums that still played in her thoughts and immediately regretted it. She grabbed her head. As if human hands could reach through bone, skin, veins, and whatever else with some magic cure and relieve the pain.

She closed her eyes and eagerly waited for sleep to take her over, but a low mumbling caused her to lazily open them again. Ignoring it was not an option. There was something about the soft melodious sound of the chants that drew her to them. She rose from the bed, stepped out into the hall, and walked in its direction, stopping at her aunt's room. Winning against the temptation to knock, she chose instead to press her ear to the warm wood in hopes to better hear what her aunt was saying. "What in the world is she doing in there?" she whispered to herself.

A warm glow lit up the one-inch opening that separated the door from the floor. She acted on the thought that entered her mind and bent down, placing her head on the floor and lined up one eye the best she could to see whatever was on the other side. To her surprise, it was her aunt's two bare feet.

The door flew open. Katelyn jumped. "Oh, Aunt Cara, you scared me."

"What do you want?"

Katelyn didn't know how to answer that. She wasn't even sure herself.

"Well," Cara growled.

"I'm sorry, I just thought I heard you talking or something."

"It's best if you get back to bed, Katelyn. See ya in the morning."

She stepped back, staring for a short time at the door her aunt had just shut in her face. A faint pain pricked at her heart, but the nasty demon that was there waiting for his big moment quickly replaced the hurt with curiosity. Katelyn stood there a minute more, thinking. It was Cara's voice that she heard alright, but that was all. Her movements, her gaze, her stance. Those were not. It was almost as if some invisible strings were controlling her motions.

Katelyn walked back to her room, closed the door, and leaned back against it. "Hmmm, either that was strange or I'm way too drunk and over thinking things." She scratched her head. "Maybe I'll talk to her about it in the morning."

Cara tip-toed down the hall and descended the stairs, being sure to skip over the squeaky one, three up from the floor. Phone calls and ticket purchases needed to be made, and the sooner the better. The trip to Hawaii was only a couple weeks away, and she wanted everything in order and ready to go.

She had just hung up from her last call when Katelyn entered the kitchen.

"Good morning, sleepy head."

"If you say so, but my head disagrees with you."

"Had a little too much fun last night, huh?"

"Not enough to forget everything," Katelyn mumbled.

"Problems don't just disappear. You know that. You have to learn to deal with them, how to confront them."

"It's fun to pretend they don't exist sometimes, though."

"True. Want something to eat?"

"No, not really."

Cara set down the pen in her hand and looked at her niece. "You are not allowed to mope around all day, feeling sorry for yourself. It's Saturday, it's a pretty day out. Let's do something."

She laughed at Katelyn's less than enthusiastic expression. "I'm serious. Go clean up. If nothing else we can weed the flower bed or something."

"Oh, now that sounds like fun."

"Man, Trevor's going to have his hands full if he decides to marry you. I feel sorry for him."

"Gee thanks, Aunt Cara. I love you too," she replied as she walked away.

Cara copied the details about the upcoming trip on a separate piece of paper for Katelyn, then went upstairs and placed it on her bed before going to her own room. "Little thoughts, planted here and there, will soon make us an unstoppable pair." Cara chimed as she held a worn book to her chest.

"It's working. Everything is working according to plan." She ran her palm across the symbol embedded in the old leather cover before placing it back in its secret place. "Soon another generation will be added to your works, my lord. Very soon."

Cara stood in front of the window and soaked up the warmth of the morning sun, then turned to make her bed. The blanket flipped through the air with a snap then fell neatly against the stuffed material below it. The narrow streams of light coming through the blinds revealed the tiny floating dust particles. She swatted at them in vain. "Stupid dust bunnies," she said while bending over to get her gym shoes, "no matter what I do you're still there."

After pulling on her shoes she went back downstairs to wait for Katelyn. Knowing her niece would be awhile gave her plenty of time to think through the different plans of action she could pursue. Although they all seemed good, she ultimately decided to stick with one she already had in place. "If it's working why change it?" she questioned. Complimenting a Burnsten had always been a good way to worm yourself into their heart. Katelyn was proof of that. Little words and phrases were spoken to drive a wedge between her and the ones she loved. Sure, it was sneaky, maybe even a little cruel...but it was working. "One step at a time."

"What did you say, Aunt Cara?"

Katelyn's sudden appearance interrupted her thoughts. "Oh nothing, just talking to myself. Anyway, ready to pull some weeds?"

"Seriously? No."

Cara grabbed her hand, "Come on."

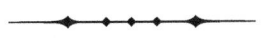

The day passed quickly, never giving Katelyn a chance to ask Cara about her strange behavior the night before. She wasn't sure if she still wanted to. Cara seemed to be back to her lighthearted self today, and she didn't want to change that. Deciding it was best to just let it go, she refocused her attention back to the unmovable weed in front of her. "Umm Cara, I need some help over here."

"Just grab a hold of it and yank it outta there."

"What do you think I've been trying to do?"

"Honestly, it looked to me like you were day dreaming. But who am I?"

Katelyn picked up a hand full of loose dirt in front of her and sent it flying in her aunt's direction, laughing as it dropped like rain on her head. "Oops, my bad."

"You will pay for that!"

"I know, but I couldn't resist."

CHAPTER FOUR

Four of heaven's best warrior angels walked shoulder to shoulder through the golden, jewel-lined palace halls, each of their twelve-foot forms covered in white and blue battle armor. Necklim, second in charge only to the Commander, had his white feathery wings tucked up behind him. Thick, rich blonde hair crowned his head and gracefully flowed down over his broad shoulders. His perfectly formed muscles were covered by taut, ivory skin and his normal, sky blue eyes, shone golden with anticipation. The sword at his side gently swayed back and forth with every determined step.

Denab walked next to Necklim. His wavy brown hair came to a rounded end just past his ears. His skin, though milky, didn't hold the same pure as snow sheen as Necklim's did. In his left hand he proudly carried his royal blue shield, the companion to the sword that hung from his right hip. Green eyes that normally peeked out through strains of hair, matched the golden blaze of his comrades.

Nolan and Sarta mirrored Necklim and Denab in their strength, but their sun-kissed skin stood in great contrast to their fellow angels'. Nolan flicked the tips of his wings impatiently as he strode in unison with the others. His long black hair had a constant shine and fell neatly against his face, highlighting his rugged and focused features. Dark eyes that matched the depths of the ocean, blazed like the embers of a hot burning fire. His mighty hand rested on top of the handle of his sword.

Sarta completed the line, walking next to the other wall. Straight, dark, brown hair rested just above his shoulders. His hazel eyes went golden as they approached the Throne Room's door and the grip around his sword's handle tightened in expectancy of their coming orders.

Necklim held open the large silver door and waited for his friends to enter before walking through himself. The praise of the angels before the Throne lifted their spirits and drew them closer to their Creator. They quickly closed the distance between Him and the door and briefly stood before lowering their heads and bowing down on a bended knee before Him.

"Nolan, I have a special mission for you. The others will wait here for your return."

Nolan stepped forward, "Yes, Lord. I am here and ready."

Nolan received his orders and disappeared.

"How your impending battle will be fought depends on the decision tonight of one lost soul. Either way, we will be ready." The Commander's words brought encouragement to the remaining three Warriors. They nodded their heads in agreement and waited patiently for their fellow angel to return.

Katelyn stood next to the window in the bedroom of her recently rented apartment in the city, a pair of shorts in her hand. The constant noise had taken her several days to get used to, but now all the different sounds played out like a city-wide orchestra – music to her ears.

"I wonder how long it'll take me to get used to crickets again once I get back to the country." The plans she'd made with Trevor to find a house out near her Aunt Cara's hadn't changed. But now wasn't the time.

She stuffed the shorts into her suitcase, zipped it shut, and placed it at the foot of her bed. "Hawaii, I'll be seeing your beautiful self in a few short days."

The clock chimed the hour and she realized she hadn't eaten yet so she made her way to the kitchen, walking past the unseen spirit with a wide smile on its face, so wide that it pulled its thin cracked lips over tiny, sharp, yellow teeth.

"This will be fun," it hissed, as it rubbed its bony fingers together.

She pulled a box from the cupboard whistling a happy tune as she set a pot full of water on the stove, unaware of the coming attack on her emotions. Within a few minutes her melodious mood had been hijacked, replaced by a deep sadness. Pain seized her heart, tightening its grip with every replayed word her mother and father had spoken over the last couple weeks.

She tried to ignore it. Tried to think of other things. It was no use. Her muscles grew tense. In an attempt to release the built up tension she rubbed the back of her neck. Yes, it had been time, past time, for her to find her own place, but the sudden and unexpected three day time period her dad had thrown upon her two weeks ago, after her weekend at Cara's, didn't seem quite fair. Somehow she managed to accomplish the task, and thanks to the help of Trevor and her aunt she had gotten her things moved in one day's time. Not that she had much.

And yes, her mother's pleas still haunted her. How different would things have been had she walked out beside her mom that night?

"Ugh. Why do I keep letting this bother me? It's so stupid. Some time away from this lovely bluegrass state will definitely do me some good."

Small pieces of uncooked pasta were sprinkled across the stove as she broke the long noodles in half, thoughts still focused on things of the past, and the family she'd grown up with that was now forever changed.

She kept the promise she'd made herself and talked to her father at least once a week, but could only stand by and watch as his relationship with his only sister went from bad to worse to nonexistent. If one of them had something to say to the other, rare as that was, Katelyn was the messenger.

Her mother on the other hand, was proving to be more difficult to keep in touch with. They had only talked once since her mom had left that night. She couldn't help but feel that her mother had all but disowned her.

Yet, through all the chaos, her friendship with Cara grew deeper and stronger. After all, she was the only family Katelyn had left that accepted her as she was. Rowdy, crazy, and living life in the fast lane. Had they really expected something different? Weren't you supposed to live your life to please yourself, not worrying about what anyone else thought – or felt. That's what Cara had done, and things were great for her. Or at least they looked to be from the outside anyway.

Not for Katelyn. Hiding her true emotions behind the mask of a fake smile was getting to be more trouble than it was worth. No matter how hard she tried to ignore her feelings, and she had, the absence of her mother from her life weighed heavily on her. Several times she'd brought it up to Cara, hoping she'd give her some wisdom on what she could do to mend the ties. But each time Cara had dismissed her concerns and told her to forget about her mom, just as she had forgotten about her. She wouldn't let herself believe that. She couldn't. How could any parent totally forget about their child? She didn't understand. Cara would no doubt still be a major issue, but at least she could try. If nothing else than for the sheer fact that neither one of them could say she hadn't.

Katelyn dumped the water and spaghetti noodles from the pot into the strainer, then placed the pot in the other side of the sink. She mixed the noodles with some homemade sauce she'd gotten from Trevor's mom, and sat down to eat.

All the recent overtime at work had seriously cut into her social life. It'd been five days since she'd seen Trevor, and her nightly check-in's with Cara dwindled down from an hour long conversation to five minutes of a quick 'hey, how are ya'. She wouldn't complain though. She liked her job as an insurance agent, and the extra money meant more she'd have to save.

She glanced at the clock as she finished cleaning up the kitchen. "I won't even have time talk with Cara tonight. It's so late, and I'm exhausted. Shower, then bed. Sounds like a plan."

Cara sat on the floor, eyes closed, breaths shallow, awaiting the next round of instructions from the head demon over the Burnsten clan – Latar. She sat on the floor, book open, potion mixed, and in charge. Or so the spirit of pride led her to believe.

A familiar pungent smell filled the room. Cara wrinkled

her nose. No matter how often her demon master paid her a visit she never got use to the smell he brought with him.

"Welcome, my lord," she whispered.

"We are close, Cara. We must fulfill our mission. There's no more time to waste. We want her on our side. You have been the greatest asset to me in your family, but our dear Katelyn will surpass even you."

The aging wooden floor bowed in front of her under Latar's large form.

"Greater than I?" Cara questioned.

"Of course she's greater than you. Our Katelyn is so important. She's another, yet bigger piece to the puzzle, and we need you to put her in place. One day, she too will be surpassed. That's how it works, Cara. You didn't forget that, did you?"

"No. I will try and do my best, my lord."

"Try?" Latar growled. "You *will* do your best. There's no other option. If you can't get her, I'll send someone else. Don't think even now, that you can't be replaced."

Cara struggled to keep her emotions in check as Latar's words registered. To be so easily excused from her family's heritage after all the work she'd put into Katelyn's turn over didn't sit well within her. But what could she do? One swipe from what she could only imagine was the gigantic figure in front of her, and she'd be gone. *Gone? Would he really manage this without me?*

"Yes, I could, and I would."

Cara opened her eyes, and for the first time in her life looked upon the form of her leader, then up into the empty, glowing, red orbs that were looking down on her. She forced herself to bury her fear, but it was to late. The smirk on Latar's face informed of her that.

"Not what you were expecting?"

Cara swallowed, but didn't respond.

"I guess not. I may not be able to read your thoughts *dear one*, but I'm an expert on reading your face. I've known you for a long time, have I not?"

"You have, my lord."

"This is what I want from you tonight. Call Katelyn, set something up for you two this weekend. Bring her here. Explain the family history and devotion to me. Reveal the book. You will have help in this matter. My servants Melti and Ackmen will be here with you, along with others. Any questions?"

Cara certainly had questions but she wasn't about to ask them, so she just shook her head. "No, my lord."

Latar's presence exited the room just as quickly as it had entered. Leaving behind someone broken, staring out into the darkness, a mere image of the in charge, self confident, girl she was known to be.

Taking her life was never something she'd given thought to before. She had everything in the world that she wanted. Latar had made sure of it. Money, men, cars, trucks, clothes. The list went on. But that was before tonight. Before the sting of a possible betrayal from the one she lived to serve. His words had cut to the very core of her, even though they shouldn't have. She knew what she was getting into. She understood how it all worked.

The flame on the candle flickered in the breeze of the fan, causing the golden vine to shine on a small, red cup in front of her. The decision had been made. She reached for the phone, dialed one last three-digit number, then let it fall to the floor before placing the rim of the cup to her lips and whispering the last words she'd ever speak. "If I'm so replaceable, my lord, then replace me."

Nolan stood silently in the shadows. The hordes of demons that had encircled Cara a short time ago had fled. It was over. There on the floor before him, lay a lost and lifeless girl. He'd waited, prayerfully for her to call out to her Creator. He would've helped ease her troubled mind if she did. But she didn't. The window had slipped away.

Nolan hid his frustration. Knowing beforehand how slim the chance of her calling out would be didn't lessen the sadness he felt inside. He wanted to protect her, to fight for her. Years had he been on alert. Waiting, watching. And now, it was over.

"Cara," he whispered.

"It's time to come home, Nolan." The Commander's voice was a comforting whisper in his ear. He flew towards it. Drew strength from it. Another battle was on the horizon. He had to be ready.

"We must carry on." The Commander's authoritative voice broke through the silence. "Katelyn and the others will need protection and guidance. Katelyn's emotions won't be stable and it'll be easier for the enemy to take over her thinking."

"Yes, Commander," they answered.

"Necklim, you will be in charge over this mission. You'll be over Cara's house, and Katelyn while she's there."

Necklim nodded his head and stepped forward as the Commander continued, "Nolan, you and Sarta are to guard

Katelyn at her home. Once she leaves there, Nolan you will join with Necklim, and Sarta you will then guard Trevor. Denab, your mission is to guard Miranda.

Each angel took formation around Necklim after they received their orders.

"Be on guard, my Warriors, and wait for my orders."

"Yes, Commander." They pulled their swords from their sheaths and lifted them above their heads, each one meeting the tip of the others, "For the Worthy!"

Necklim arrived at his post moments after leaving the Throne Room. The old farm house, to anyone else, would have appeared dark and empty. Not to Necklim. He knew better. It was dark yes, but empty – no.

He swiftly lowered his battle-ready form behind the tree line just south of his post and watched intently between it, the fading orange sky with its increasing dark clouds and smell of rain, and the growing number of vile spirits heading in his direction.

A loud shriek pierced his ears, grabbing not only his attention, but the attention of all the spirits that were yards in front of him. They quieted down and looked off towards the north, while he did the same.

Their leader?

Every demon large and small bowed before the giant dark figure as he landed in front of them, two other good sized demons with him.

A clash of thunder preceded a steady rainfall, and in the fleeting glow of the bright light that followed, their opponent was revealed; he was big and had horns on either side of his head that curved forward, their pointed ends coming to a stop just beside his eyes.

Latar.

A green mist flowed from between his teeth as he questioned the gathering in front of him, "What happened here tonight?"

No evil figure had an answer. Latar flapped his leathery wings in indignation.

Nolan's long black hair fell gently on his shoulders as he and Sarta quietly landed on Katelyn's roof. They scanned the night sky before turning their attention to their charge.

"No evidence of the enemy," Nolan whispered.

"That's strange," Sarta replied.

"Yes, it is," Nolan agreed. "You stay here and keep watch. I'm going to go check on her. The call should be coming in soon." Nolan turned and closed his eyes, then continued, "I want to be the one there when she answers it."

He made his way, unseen and unannounced, into Katelyn's room and stood just inside the door, hand on his sword – ever ready. There in the corner she stood, turning this way and that, looking over her appearance in the full length mirror in front of her. "I'm putting on so much weight. How can Trevor even stand to look at me?"

The coal colored mist that surrounded her laughed. "Shall I continue, or would you like a turn?" he said to the feathery snake-like spirit that had slithered out from under the bed, and now stood behind her, its wispy fingers ready to plunge their three inch daggers straight into her heart awakening a fear she'd never known before.

Nolan stepped out from the shadows, causing the puny demons to shriek and cautiously move back away from their target. Uneasiness and confusion were written all over their faces.

"What are you doing here?" they hissed.

Nolan remained unmoved and quiet as he watched their eyes dart back and forth between him and Katelyn. She wasn't just their target, she was his charge.

He focused on Katelyn as she pulled back the covers on her bed and laid down, unaware of not only the menacing spirits around her, but of the events that would shortly take place.

He wasn't unaware. He tightened his tan fingers around the top of his sword – and waited.

"Another late night...great. I'll be crabby in the morning." Katelyn mindlessly tossed down the remote after shutting off the television. She had just pulled up the covers and closed her eyes, and started reasoning with her brain to take the night off when her phone rang.

"Ugh." She glared at the soft glow that was coming from her nightstand. "Aunt Cara, that better not be you. I know we haven't talked today, but it's late and I need to get some sleep." She reached over, picked up the phone and focused on the number that was displayed on the tiny screen. "Hmm, don't know who you are," she said as she went to lay the phone back down, trying to fight off the urge in her gut to answer the stranger on the other end. She couldn't.

"Hello?" She said unsure, giving a second thought to her bright idea.

"Ms. Burnsten?"

"Yes, this is she."

"Ms. Burnsten, this is Officer Nagel with the Green Hill,

Kentucky Police Department. I regret to inform you that Cara Burnsten has passed away."

"What?" Katelyn questioned, not sure she had heard the man on the other end of the line correctly. "There has to be a mistake," she said, heart beating against her chest.

"There is no mistake, miss. We're not sure what happened, there will be an investigation, although it looks self-inflicted and like there was no foul play. Your number was the only one we found in her address book that had family written next to it. I know this probably isn't the best time, but we'll need you to come in and ID her. You can wait until the morning if you prefer."

The phone slid from Katelyn's hand and landed on the floor with a thud. *Suicide?* The last thing she remembered hearing was the faint sound of the officer's voice by her feet. Her body shook. Moisture formed a blurry covering over her eyes. She blinked and it made its way down her cheek – increasing in frequency. "This can't be true. Someone is playing a joke. A very cruel joke." Her stomach cramped, forcing her to make a dash for the restroom across the hall.

She kept her head hung over the white oval shaped bowl until her mid-section had calmed down enough for her to move. Once she was sure it had, she lowered herself to the floor and leaned back against the tub. The coolness of the porcelain coming through her shirt felt good against her warm form. "This has to be a bad dream. It just has to be."

She grabbed hold of the skin on her arm and pinched as hard as she could, then rubbed the red mark that had been left behind. "No, I definitely felt that." She pulled her legs to her chest, wrapped her arms tightly around them, and rested her head on her knees. Images of her aunt's lifeless body lying on the floor took over her thoughts. She tried to stop them. Tried to think of something else, but her mind wouldn't let her. No matter how hard she tried. Closing her eyes didn't help. It only made the images clearer. "Oh, Aunt Cara." She whispered through her sobs. "What happened?"

The next morning arrived too soon. Unwillingly, Katelyn pushed herself up off the floor, took a deep breath, and walked back across the hall. She stopped in front of the phone still lying where it had fallen the night before, and stared at it before finally picking it up, the whole time dreading the call she knew she had to make. She punched in the numbers, placed the phone to her ear, sighed and then whispered, "For the last time, my dear father, I get to be the go-between for you and Aunt Cara." Absentmindedly she asked for the Lord's help while waiting for her father to answer.

Nolan seized the tiny window she had unknowingly opened and began to speak words of comfort to her. He stood, strong and tall, stretched out his wings and wrapped them around the trembling young woman in front of him.

The demons growled and hissed their frustration, but quickly shut up with one glance of the glowing embers in the eyes of their enemy.

"You can do this, Katelyn. You will get through this. Trust in God, His love for you is far beyond any human comprehension. Trust in Him. Believe in Him. He is here for you."

Katelyn hadn't heard Nolan's words, but was taken aback at the peace that began to envelope her. "How odd."

"Katelyn, is that you? What's odd?"

"Umm, yes Dad, it's me. Listen I have to tell you something about Aunt Cara, and before you interrupt or hang up, please just listen."

"What is it?"

"Cara's gone, Dad," she whispered through a shaky voice. "She died last night."

She remained silent for several minutes, giving time for what she had said to sink in.

"Dad, are you there? Did you hear me?"

"Yes, I heard you. Text me the details for the arrangements. I have to go." The line went silent.

"Go figure. That's just like you!" She screamed out into what she thought was an empty room. "I don't know why I expected anything different," she said in disgust. Her knuckles turned a shade of white as she tightened her fists. "You were never there when she needed you. Why change now?" She slammed her phone down on the nightstand and walked over to the window. She pulled the curtains back and looked out at the cloud-filled sky. Her fresh tears fell as fast and numerous as the raindrops on the opposite side of the windowpane.

———◆ ◆ ◆ ◆———

Katelyn hung up the phone. It was the third message she'd left for her mom, this one containing the information about the funeral. She knew it was a long shot but she'd hoped her mom would be there, if nothing else at least to bring her some comfort. But the unreturned phone calls offered little hope. Maybe she really had disowned her.

Five days had passed, Katelyn stood next to her aunt's grave protectively wrapped in Trevor's embrace. There was no fighting back the tears today. Today, she would let them flow. She wiped the wetness from her cheeks and glanced up at the sea of people that had come to say goodbye to her aunt. If it wasn't for Leah's height Katelyn might have missed her mom altogether as she blended in with everyone.

"Mom?" she whispered

She tugged on the sleeve of Trevor's shirt and pointed in the direction she'd been looking. "Trevor, is that my mom?"

Trevor leaned up on his toes, then looked back at Katelyn. "Yes, I think it's your mom."

A slight smile found its way across her lips. Knowing her mom was there dulled the ache in heart, but only for a short time.

Katelyn felt a gentle pull on her arm. The service had ended. "Come on, let's go," Trevor said gently.

Sorrow grabbed onto her and wouldn't let go. Leaving there would mean it was final. It would mean her aunt was really gone. It would mean she'd have to say goodbye forever.

"Why?"

Trevor moved around in front of her and cupped her face in his hands. He wiped the tears from her cheeks with his thumbs and kissed her forehead. "It'll be alright, Katelyn," he whispered.

"No. I don't think it will." She stared in front of her, right through him, into a world she didn't recognize anymore. A world filled with uncertainty. A world filled with pain. "Will my heart ever heal?"

"Yes, Katelyn, you will heal. The memory will always be with you, but the pain will lessen over time." Trevor wrapped his arm around her and led her to the car.

"I'm not so sure I believe that."

"You might not right now, but you'll see."

"What will I do without her, Trev?"

"The same thing you did with her – live. That's what she would want you to do. Remember the good times you all had together. The laughter, the joy."

"It won't be easy."

"You're right, it won't be. But you're a strong woman, my little Katelyn Mae...flower." He glanced in her direction and saw a tiny, yet forced smile.

"That never fails," he said.

"Never fails to what? Show how silly you are?"

Trevor laughed. "No, it never fails to make you smile."

"I just had to be born in May and blessed with that as my middle name as well. Thanks, Mom and Dad." Katelyn turned in a circle, the memory of seeing her mom now in the forefront of her mind. "Mom, where's my mom?"

"I'm right here."

Katelyn turned then fell into the soft, protecting arms of her mother. "I'm so glad you came. It means so much to me," she sobbed.

"I love you, Katelyn."

She stood up and straightened her dress. "Then why haven't you taken my calls, or at least called me back?"

"Forgive me. That will all change."

Katelyn shook her head. A tiny ray of hope flickered in her eyes. "Okay."

"I have to go. I'll call you later."

"Okay, Mom."

"So, would you like me to take you to your dad's? Ya know, for the gathering. It might do you some good to be around familiar faces."

"Trev, you and I both know that's not true." She sighed. "But I guess I should make an appearance. I honestly don't want to though. I'd like to run as far away from this town as possible."

"I know you would." Trevor quickly glanced in her direction.

"Promise me that we won't stay too long."

"I promise."

"Thank you for coming with me, Trevor. It means a lot to me."

"By your side is where I belong, Katelyn. It's where I want to be."

Katelyn fiddled with the strap on her purse as they drove up her father's driveway. Anywhere but here is where she wanted to be.

Trevor put the car in park, then handed her a tissue from the console.

"Thanks," she said as she pulled down the visor. "I'm a mess, I can't go in there. Just look at me." She faced him.

"No, you're not. You look like someone that has just lost their best friend. Which is the truth. Besides, the people in there, ya know, your family and friends, they don't care what you look like. They care about you."

Katelyn grabbed the blush and eyeliner from out of her purse and re-applied them before giving her attention to anything else. "I suppose you're right." She flipped the visor back to its original spot, leaned towards Trevor, and laid her head on his shoulder. "Not too long?"

"Whenever you're ready, we'll go."

"Let's get this over with then."

She had just stepped out of the car when she heard a voice from her past call out her name. She turned around.

"Oh, Katelyn, I'm so sorry to hear about your aunt. Is there anything I can do?"

She stood there in shock as she came eye to eye with her long lost best friend. Well, ex-best friend. "Thank you, Miranda, but no. There's nothing *you* or anyone else can do."

Miranda handed her a business card. "Here's my number. In case you ever want or need to talk."

Katelyn politely took the card from Miranda's extended hand and shoved it into her front pocket. Her eyes narrowed. "I don't need it, but thanks."

Without saying anything more, Katelyn turned and walked away, leaving a confused Trevor standing there by himself. "I'm sorry, she's just really upset right now."

"There's no need to apologize. I'm just glad I was able to see her. She's going through a hard time. Not to mention I'm probably the last person she expected to see today. Well, I must be going."

"Yes, of course," Trevor stuck out his hand, "it was nice to meet you..."

"Miranda."

"I'm Trevor, Katelyn's boyfriend. It was nice to meet you, Miranda."

"Likewise, Trevor."

Katelyn got herself together before walking through her father's front door. One by one she was greeted by people offering condolences and support. She couldn't remember a time when she'd ever uttered the words 'thank you' so much in such a short amount of time, but her mind was on something – someone else. To her surprise it wasn't her aunt, or even her father, but the girl she'd just come face to face with outside. The girl that she hadn't seen or talked to in years.

She quickly made her way through the group of people, into the kitchen and pulled out a chair to sit down in. It screeched as she dragged it across the wooden floor and she curled her lip. The last thing she wanted to do was draw more attention to herself. She leaned up against the table, resting her chin on the palm of her hand and thought about the once tiny red-headed girl with purple rimmed glasses and freckles that covered her cheeks and stretched across her nose. Miranda's brother used to tease her and said it looked as if she'd stood in front of a screen door. Katelyn knew it was all in good fun, but she caught a glimpse of the pain in her friend's expression more than once.

All the taunting had ceased by the time their senior year rolled around. Miranda was no longer the skinny girl with no shape to her form. Her long legs stood her a full two inches taller than Katelyn's five foot four height, and those geeky glasses were a thing of the past. Truth be told she was a little jealous of her friend. The ugly duckling had turned into a beautiful swan, leaving her the same old *plain Jane* she had always been.

That wasn't the only change that took a hold of Miranda that year. Something had changed her heart. She was extending kindness where any normal teenage girl would be plotting and seeking revenge on her once hurtful classmates. Katelyn stood in the shadows as Miranda's grace seemed to propel her forward. No matter what Miranda applied her hands to, it flourished.

Katelyn shuddered as she replayed their last conversation in her mind.

"Hi Katelyn!" Miranda yelled above the many voices that filled the crowded hallway.

Katelyn turned and started walking in the other direction, pretending she hadn't heard her friend. Her plan hadn't worked though, Miranda now stood right beside her.

"Hey, didn't you hear me?"

She didn't even dignify her with an answer.

"Okay, well, anyway. I was wondering if you'd like to come with me somewhere fun this weekend?"

"Oh, and where would that be, your Bible-thumping, holier-than-thou church?" She knew she had caught her friend off guard, but at the time she didn't care. She was so sick and resentful of the peace and happiness her friend now had. "No thank you. I wouldn't be caught dead in one of those buildings." Her eyes became narrow slits as she stared at the girl in front of her, before walking off.

Her friend's whispered words barely reached her ears. "No, I was going to ask you to the Dunk and Dive."

Katelyn's steps had slowed, but only for a moment. She had refused to let her shock be made known to anyone, let alone Miranda. Refuge was just around the corner anyway. She leaned up against the cool brick and shook her head, "The Dunk and Dive. You and your big mouth! Where did that comment come from anyway?" She sighed. "It was just the Dunk and Dive. How could I have been so cruel?"

Months of unanswered phone calls, texts, and just plain staying clear of Miranda, finally left Katelyn with one less friend. Her actions that day, mixed with pride and unforgiveness, had caused her to not just step, but leap over a friendship line. She couldn't go back. That she knew for sure. Things would never be the same, and so she buried it, and moved on.

CHAPTER FIVE

Trevor's persistence had finally paid off, leaving a mere thirty minutes for Katelyn to get herself together. It was the first night since Cara's funeral, two weeks ago, that she agreed to leave her aunt's house. She had practically moved into it. Her days had been spent searching for answers to Cara's unexpected death, yet she was getting nowhere. Trevor had voiced his concern multiple times about her "letting him down easy". Even so, she wasn't crazy about going out. But she couldn't argue the fact that a change of scenery would be nice, not to mention some fresh air. Being cooped up in Cara's home, without her, had started to take its toll on her in many ways, her mind being one of them.

"Maybe a night out won't be so bad after all," she said, sliding open the door to her closet. A selection of outfits hung in front of her. Deciding to go with something simple, she pulled a blue, long sleeved dress from its resting place and watched as the hanger lightly swayed back and forth. "I guess this will have to do."

She slipped it over her head and then bent down to pick out the final touch to her ensemble – shoes. Her feet protested as she crammed them into a slender pair of wedged sandals. "The things a woman goes through to look nice, it's downright ridiculous sometimes. Why'd I let him talk me in to going out anyway? It would've been just as easy for him to bring something here." She plopped down on the bed and secured the last strap of her shoe in place. "Oh, right, fresh air."

She rubbed her lips together, smearing in the soft rose color that had just been applied to them, then made one last turn in front of the full length mirror.

"This is as good as it gets," she mumbled making her way down the stairs.

A chime echoed throughout the old wooden structure and her prior feelings and complaints were replaced with anticipation. "Who knows, I just might have a little fun tonight after all."

She opened the door and her heart fluttered in her chest. She couldn't help but obey the invisible strings that pulled on the corners of her mouth. There in front of her stood Trevor's muscular form covered in a white t-shirt, blue jeans, boots, and a black Stetson hat, with a collection of yellow and white wildflowers clutched in his hand.

Why after two years does this cowboy still give me butterflies?

"Hey, Trevor." She took the flowers and walked to the kitchen to hide the flush of warmth on her cheeks. "These are very pretty. Thank you."

"Not as pretty as you," he said as he spun her around.

"Oh, Trev, stop that. You're gonna make me blush. Besides, I need to get these," she gently waved the flowers between them, "in some water."

"Looks like you're already blushing to me. And besides, you don't have to worry about those." He took the bouquet and laid it on the counter. "I didn't want to show up with nothing so I picked 'em out of the side yard before I left. They're nothing fancy."

Held captive by his inviting green eyes, she silently scolded herself for letting the all too natural feelings he caused course through her body. *Get a hold of yourself, you know better!*

It was useless. She lost all control when he looked at her that way.

Does he even realize what he does to me? And if he does, how dare he!

A smile crossed her lips as she pushed him away. "They are too fancy, and need to be put in some water. Will you grab the vase under the sink for me?"

Trevor opened the door, moved a couple things aside and grabbed the clear glass container. "Here ya go, ma'am."

"Thanks." She let the water run until it was just right, filled the vase half full, placed the flowers inside and then set it on the table. "There, doesn't that look nice?"

"Yeah, I suppose it does."

"I think it does," she said while she slid her finger back and forth over a tiny missing part of the table she had just noticed. "Hmmm, I wonder where that came from?" Try as she might she couldn't recall something being set on the table that could have chipped it like that. She leaned in closer.

"What are you talking about?"

She pointed in the direction of the very obvious lighter mark on the table, "This right here."

The feel of Trevor's hand around hers brought little comfort to her anxious mind as he moved it aside.

"This?" Trevor titled his head to get a better a look.

"Yeah, that," she whispered.

"It's just a scratch."

She knew that, but still couldn't shake the feeling that

somehow, it was more than *just* a scratch. This out of place mark strongly resembled the tip of something very sharp, the tip of something claw-like. She took a deep breath, closed her eyes and tried, with little success, to steady her shaking hands.

She wondered what Trevor must think of her now. She'd never shown him this side of herself. The side that could so easily be taken over and gripped by fear. *He probably thinks I'm nuts. All this fuss over something so insignificant.*

"Why does that have you so upset?"

"I don't know. I'm just, just losing my mind – I think."

"See, I told you that you needed some time away from this house," he smiled.

Agreeing with him was hard, especially when she knew he was right, and she didn't want him to be.

"I don't know, Trevor."

His calloused fingers caused a shiver to run up her spine as they rubbed against her soft skin and enclosed her hand, moving it away from the centerpiece. "Come on," he said. "Let's go."

She started to protest, but froze as the hair on the back of her neck stood on end. *Not again.* Heaviness filled the air. If Trevor felt it, he didn't show it.

She looked over his shoulder as a shadowy figure suddenly appeared in front of the main entrance. Then disappeared.

Yep, I'm losing my mind for sure.

She tightened her grip on Trevor's hand. "Yeah, let's get out of here." She grabbed her purse off the table and opened the door. "After you."

Katelyn sat on the edge of the bed on the second floor of her aunt's home. She slipped off the shoes that had restricted her toes all evening and rubbed her feet. Images raced through her mind of what she had seen over Trevor's shoulder on the porch as she hugged him goodbye. Up until now the sightings and feelings only happened inside the house. "I've been experiencing way too much weird stuff around here."

She hummed the tune of one of her favorite songs in the hopes of distracting herself. It didn't work. "It couldn't be real, could it? Those things don't really exist, do they?" She rubbed at the faint pounding in her head while shuddering at the mental picture that had taken over her thoughts.

"No, they aren't real. They can't be. They just can't be. I don't know what all this stuff is. Maybe it's my mind playing tricks on me, heck, maybe it's the pain I've pushed away finally claiming its rightful place at the forefront of my mind. I don't know. But real, this stuff, no."

She dug her toes into the soft, plush, carpet and turned her attention to the five by seven frame that held her favorite picture of her and her aunt. It had been taken three years ago on one of their yearly trips. Their sun-kissed skin had made the white shorts and neon bikini tops stand out even more.

She smiled at the memory of Cara's gift – a tiny pink bikini. She had taken it from her aunt's hand and twirled it around aimlessly in front her, wide-eyed. Cara's style had always been a bit flaunty. *"If you've got it, you might as well flaunt it,"* she'd say.

"Well," Katelyn said aloud as she traced her finger along the edge of the frame. "What do you think of it all, Aunt

45

Cara?" She longed to hear an answer from her aunt, even though she knew it was not possible.

Katelyn reveled in the fact that her dad's sister was only seven years older than her. Cara had been like a big sister and mother all wrapped up in one. No matter what she needed or wanted Cara saw to it that she got it.

She wiped away a tear before it could roll down her cheek, betraying the pain she tried to keep bottled up inside. Hiding her emotions had never been such a task before.

She returned her gaze to the picture she held in her hand and ran her slender finger over the two faces that stared back at her before returning it to its rightful place beside her bed. "I miss you so much, Aunt Cara."

"Maybe a bath would help me to relax, and take my mind off things. It's been awhile since I've just sat, not thinking about anything." She pulled the long, thick, black tresses off her shoulders and twisted them around before placing a clip in them to hold them up.

The rings jingled as she pushed the shower curtain to the side. A crystal-looking knob gave way under the pressure of her hand, releasing the spits and sputters of cold water. She let it run a little longer, then held her arm under the flow of the warming liquid and watched as it streamed from the silver spout and plopped into its metal holding place. "Just right," she said and pushed in the plug.

Small drops splashed up against her leg as she placed one foot in, followed by the other. She sat down then leaned back resting her head against the shell-shaped bath pillow, enjoying the quiet and escape of the wet cocoon around her. "Yes, this is what I needed."

She hadn't realized how much time passed until she noticed her wrinkled fingertips. "I suppose I should get out before all of me ends up looking like this." She sat up and pulled the chain, releasing the barrier between the water and the holes on the other side. It gurgled and swirled around before disappearing down the drain.

After securing the soft green material that had once hung on the bar next to the tub around her, she grabbed a hand towel from under the sink and began wiping the fog from the mirror. She stared at her reflection for a moment and then shook her head. The once perfect make-up was a smudged mess, thanks to the warm steam of the bath. She dampened the cloth and wiped around her eyes several times before laying it down. "That will just have to do for tonight. I'm too tired to mess with it anymore."

The dresser drawer let out a high pitched sound as she pulled it from its place. A pair of tattered cotton shorts and an extra long T-shirt were tossed in the direction of the bed behind her. Sleep was after all, about comfort.

She dressed and got into bed. One uncovered foot dangled off the edge. She stared out in the darkness, eyes growing heavy. There wouldn't be a fight to stay awake tonight. For the first time since her aunt's death, sleep would be welcomed.

CHAPTER SIX

Ackmen's large black figure stood silently in the shadows of the moon-lit room. His long paper-thin wings tucked up behind his back came to a point just above his head. Cracked narrow lips formed a vile grin as a yellow smoke was exhaled from his mouth, lingering like a wispy cloud through-out the room.

His eyes glowed with hatred as he stared at the frail human who lay asleep only a few feet away, unaware of his sinister presence.

"This will be easy," he whispered in to the air.

He unfolded his wings and with several flaps disappeared through the ceiling, coming to a stop on the shingled rooftop above. He strolled back and forth while he waited for Melti to arrive, keeping a close listen for any noise out of the ordinary.

The mission of drawing Katelyn in would no doubt catch the enemies' eye. That was not something they could take lightly.

Ackmen stared out over the fields, so lost in his own thoughts that he hadn't heard Melti land behind him. He turned to make another pass and was taken by surprise at the slighter bigger demon standing in his path.

"Melti. I didn't hear you."

"You need to pay attention. If I can sneak up on you so can the enemy. I've received word that they have been seen a couple of times near Katelyn. Not since she's been here, though. We must be vigilant and not back down. We must stand strong on the ground we've gained. Losing it is not an option. If they were around her elsewhere, you can be sure they are around here too."

Ackmen knew Melti spoke the truth. Just the thought of the heavenly angels making their presence known repulsed him, causing a sick feeling of dread to flow through his body.

"Who's watching her?"

Melti's voice was low as the name rolled off his skinny ashen tongue. "Nolan."

Ackmen voiced his concern, "If Nolan's around, that means Necklim isn't far." He shook his head. His feeling of fear was not unfounded. They'd all had the great honor, as some saw it, of being in combat with Necklim and his army before. There were many causalities every time. How the three of them had always kept their heads attached to their shoulders was a mystery none of them could answer.

"You are correct," Melti agreed.

A quiver ran down the boney spine of Ackmen, the words of Necklim at their last battle fresh on his mind. "You will cease to exist if we should meet again."

Melti's low growl snapped him back to the present. "Do you have anything to report?"

"An opening arose tonight. One we'd been waiting for. So I took it."

"Do tell," Melti prodded

"I gave our little sleeping beauty a glimpse of the unseen world around her."

"Continue."

"I revealed myself tonight on the porch as she hugged Trevor goodbye. I was standing behind him, fingers curled and wings stretched out. My strength grew as I sensed her fear. I have no doubt that she'll be just as easy to control as her dearly departed aunt was. If nothing else, using her deepest darkest fears against her." Ackmen's words resembled the hissing of a curled snake ready to strike as they flowed off his tongue.

Melti's sinister laugh lingered out across the flat land in front of them. "Even with the enemy's presence we'll press on. We have much to accomplish in a short amount of time. Katelyn's someone we can't afford to lose. Her part in this plan is too important. Be careful not to scare her too much, we want her to come to us, not run away. All Necklim needs to disrupt our plans is a tiny ray of hope to flicker within her. We don't want her to investigate the goodness of the world, however little there may be left in it. We want her to welcome and accept the hatred. Then we can use her – mightily."

"Yes, Melti."

A strong gust of wind swirled around Ackmen as Melti leaped into the air. With his partner now off in the distance, Ackmen returned to his post in the room below. Satisfied with the meeting he let the memory of the delicate face, filled with apprehension play over and over again in his malicious mind.

Trevor's mom sat in her favorite dark green, wing back chair next to the bay window in the living room, reading her Bible just as she had every night for the past twenty years. She was praying God's word over her family, and over Katelyn. She'd asked the Lord to guide her prayers. To lead her to the passages that needed to be read and prayed. One kept coming to her mind.

"We do not wrestle against flesh and blood, but against spiritual forces in the heavenly realms." She tapped her finger at the end of the verse. "Okay, Lord, something's going on. What is it?"

Sarta stood next to her, shielding her from the prying eyes of the figures outside the window.

"You have no claim here. This family, this house, and this land belong to God. Be gone!"

Sarta watched as the figures backed away, becoming encircled by the darkness.

Necklim stood off in the edge of the trees next to the old farm house, every bit of him hidden from the enemies' sight above. He watched as the gruesome demonic figure flew from the rooftop into the night. He shook his head and rested his hand on the hilt of his sword, ready to strike at the sound of the battle cry. "Lord, when You're ready, so am I."

Necklim glanced around several times making sure they were alone before he raised the glowing white sword above his head, signaling for the meeting to start. Across the field, in the outline of the sporadic trees several more lights shone brightly against the blanket of darkness.

He crossed the neatly manicured lawn to the barn and appeared through the closed door. Nolan, Sarta, and Denab gave their greetings as he entered. "Good evening, Necklim," they called out in unison.

"Good evening everyone."

"Is there any news yet on the battle for Katelyn?" Nolan asked.

Necklim patted Nolan's shoulder. He knew how much this human meant to his friend but he couldn't speed up God's perfect timing, even if he wanted to. "Not yet my friend, hopefully soon."

Necklim stood in the middle of the barn. The rest of the angels now present had formed a circle around him.

"As I was just informing Nolan," he glanced over at his fellow comrade, then back towards Warriors in front of him. "I haven't received any new orders. So we will continue watching over Katelyn from a distance. Unfortunately, the closeness we have to her is dwindling. This barn and the outlying trees are about as close as we can get right now."

He gave a nod in the direction of a fellow angel that had not been assigned a human charge, "Ezera, see if you can find some prayer warriors nearby. Take their names to the Throne and ask for the Almighty's permission to have their hearts be burdened to pray. We've lost the covering of the garden around the house, and the field. The driveway is debatable right now. The closer we are able to get, the better."

Necklim saw the determination in the angel's features as he straightened his form and squared his shoulders.

"Yes, consider it done, Commander." Ezera replied.

"We must be watchful though," Necklim reminded them. "I have a feeling things are going to get ugly."

The angels shook their heads in agreement.

"Let's bring this meeting to a close then. Remember to stay hidden. Our enemy knows we are around, but that doesn't mean they need to know our exact locations, or how many of us are here, unless necessary."

They raised their swords and looked to the sky, "For the

Worthy." They each nodded their farewells and returned to their posts as Ezera left for his mission. All except Nolan.

Necklim noticed his friend's slumped shoulders. "Take heart, Nolan. The Father's timing is always perfect. Even if we don't understand it."

"I know. Many battles we have fought together. Each was important in its own right. They were fought in the hopes of bringing the human to the saving knowledge of our God's wonderful grace. Some we lost, but many we were victorious in. This one though, this one is different for me – closer to me."

"I know, my friend. I know. Her decision will be made soon."

Nolan nodded his head. "Yes, it will. I just hope she makes the right one."

Necklim returned to his post on the north side of the house after watching Nolan return to his on the south. His thoughts filled with the girl inside and the demon watching over her. He knew Ackmen. He had fought against him before. He knew his tactics, the way he worked. He didn't like it. "When my, Lord? When?" He watched for movement in the sky, attentively listening for his Master's voice.

◆ ◆ ◆ ◆

Denab returned to his charge – Miranda. He stood next to her bed and watched as she tossed and turned. He knew the Lord was laying it on her heart to pray. Ezera's request had been answered. He spread out his wings and surrounded her, keeping her concealed from the enemy's sight and waited patiently. The Lord was wanting more than just her sleep-filled prayers tonight.

Finally Miranda sat up and pulled the covers over her lap making them into a big lump on her legs before grabbing her Bible and notebook off the nightstand.

She wiped the sleep from her eyes, and opened the book that she had lain on the make-shift cover desk. "Okay, Lord, I don't know what's going on, but you do. Lead me to the scriptures to pray."

A sudden heaviness filled her heart. She jotted down the scriptures that popped into her mind, one after another. She flipped back and forth between the thin, crinkly pages until every scripture had been read aloud and prayed. Yet the heaviness remained. She took a deep breath and refocused her attention to the scriptures in front of her. Again, she turned the pages, stopping at each verse. She opened her notebook to a blank piece of paper and began to write. Each verse was copied word for word.

"Okay, what do these verses have in common?" She read over each one again while taking mental notes. "Protection, and salvation," she said. "Father, give me a name, give me a face, give me something I can put in these scriptures."

Miranda let the praise, worship, and pleadings that filled her heart flow out through her lips in a hushed tone. It wasn't until she opened her eyes that she realized over an hour had passed. She closed them again, and sat quiet before the Lord. A name was whispered into her heart.

"Katelyn."

CHAPTER SEVEN

Katelyn wiped away the moisture forming on her brow and tossed the covers to the side, watching as they slid off the bed and onto the floor. "Ugh. Why can't I sleep? Is that too much to ask for?"

She flopped her long legs over the edge of the bed, stood up, made her way to the bathroom and picked up the washcloth that she had laid on the edge of the sink a couple hours earlier. She stuck it under the faucet, interrupting the water's smooth flow. She noted the difference, as slight as it was, in the weight as the semi-dry towel soaked up the cold liquid. "Much like life I guess. The more you take in the heavier your burdens get."

She twisted the water-filled cloth, wringing out every last drop, then placed it on the nap of her neck and headed to the kitchen. "Here I am trying to get my aunt's affairs in order and from the moment I walked into this house I've been nothing but a mess."

She filled a cup with some ice-cold sweet tea and gulped it down. "And here I am talking to myself again. Just great. Maybe I need to consider staying at my place for a while; get away from the loneliness of being here."

She set the cup down and rubbed the cloth over her face,

resting it for a moment on her forehead before placing it back on her neck. A loud thump came from her aunt's room, disrupting her contemplation. She turned her head and stood motionless, heart pounding. "Great, just great. Nice to know you pick the fear instead of flight response," she mumbled. "It's an old house, though. They come with all kinds of strange noises, right? Yeah, that's what I'm going to go with. Strange noises."

Having finally convinced herself that was the truth, she ignored the sound that had caused a brief moment of anxiety to rush through her, and decided to go back to bed. That lasted until she made it half way across the kitchen when she heard it again. No matter how hard she tried to move, nothing would budge, thanks in part to the unseen spirit of fear that entangled itself around her feet and latched onto her legs, freezing her into place. She was like a deer caught in the headlights, knowing impending doom was only seconds away, yet not being able to move out of its path.

She dug deep. Deep into her inner most being and grabbed onto what she thought was for sure her last ounce of courage and forcefully scooted her foot across the floor. Inch by inch she closed the distance between her and the door. Dragging the demon along with her.

Her hand reached the knob just as another thump rang out – louder, closer.

"Where do you think you're going?" A voice growled. The hot breath from the unknown thing behind her rushed up against her neck, accompanied by the foul smell of rotten eggs.

"Well?"

Katelyn couldn't have answered if she wanted to. Every part of her was paralyzed.

Ackmen commanded the spirit of fear to release her, "She'll be back," he said.

Reluctantly the tiny demon slowly removed his claws from Katelyn's legs and unwrapped himself from her. "You're no fun," the spirit complained.

"You can have all the fun you want later. We cannot push the issue right now."

Katelyn counted to three, flung the door open, and ran. The gravel cut into her bare feet, leaving small smudges of blood on the sharp rocks underneath them. She winced for a moment at the pain but kept running, staying focused on the soft green grass a few feet ahead of her.

Evil laughter filled the darkness as the door slammed shut, sending a sudden jerk throughout her body. For a brief moment she wanted to turn around and confront whatever disgusting thing that was. What right did it have anyway? Taking over her aunt's house like that. It wasn't invited – was it?

Reaching the tree line she ran behind the first big, solid tree she found and leaned up against it. The rough bark scratched against her skin through the thin T-shirt. She fought to catch her breath, clutching at the searing pain in her side. Doubled over, she propped herself up with one hand on her knee and pulled her hair out of the way with the other one. She knew what was coming. As much as she'd try and fight against it, she'd lose. She always did. Her body shook as a salty taste filled her mouth. Tears streamed down her face as she stared at the dinner she'd eaten only hours before now lying on the ground in front of her.

She stayed there in that hunched over position for a while longer. Concentrating on each inhaled and exhaled breath. She had to calm down. She had to compose herself.

The situation called for it, whether she wanted to or not. She was going to have to face it, even though she wanted to run away from it all. The house, Cara's death, the pain, her unmerciful father. All of it. Yet, she couldn't. A nagging deep within wouldn't let her.

She stood up slowly and rested for a moment before sticking her head out from behind her hiding place. A crease ran along her forehead as her eyebrows bunched up, "Wha..." Her eyes had to be deceiving her. She blinked several times before looking back in the direction of her aunt's home. A rapid flash of light appeared behind every curtain. When it finally stopped each window visible was glowing with a warm yellow hue.

While still staring in unbelief a dark movement in the living room caught her attention. She squinted her eyes trying to get a better look. "Is that a shadow? This is crazy!" She shook her head. "I'm starting to question my own sanity. What am I going to do? I can't go back in that place....I won't!"

She returned her gaze to the small group of trees in front of her. "But where can I go?" She stuffed her hand in her pocket, then the other. "Great, I don't even have my phone!"

Tears threatened to roll down her cheeks. She fought them off. "Now is not the time to cry. You've got to pull yourself together, Katelyn." She peeked around the tree once more, and focused her mind on what she had to do. There was no other choice. All her things were in there.

"My money – my clothes – my phone. She looked down at her exposed bare feet in the moonlight. "My shoes."

Dull flashes entered Necklim's peripheral vision, distracting him just enough to draw his attention away from the girl hidden behind the tree. *What are you up to now, Ackmen?* He straightened his position, reaching his full height, and locked his knees. Two feet, wrapped in golden sandals, were securely planted to the ground beneath them. He flicked his wings slightly back and forth in anticipation as he gripped the handle of his sword.

The lights finally ceased their flashing and remained on. Yet an eerie silence filled the humid night air. "Silence is hardly ever something good when it comes to Ackmen. I don't like this," Necklim said to himself.

He glanced back at the girl that stood a few feet away. Her body, to human eyes was concealed by the darkness, but not to his and certainly not Ackmen's. The confusion etched upon her face drew out the desire in him to fight, to protect, to defend. He couldn't though, not yet. He must wait for the command from the Throne. "Oh, Lord. How long?"

"Necklim."

He turned towards his comrade.

"What is he doing in there?" Nolan asked.

Necklim shook his head. He didn't want to voice all the thoughts that were racing through his mind. "I'm not sure, Nolan. If I had to guess, I'd say he's playing on her emotions and her fear. He, as well as I, got a glimpse of it earlier this evening when he revealed himself." Necklim hated to admit what he had seen earlier, but knew Nolan, as his second in command, needed to know what they might be up against.

Nolan shook his head. "Exactly how he pulled in the first Burnsten. Fear, obedience, and then you're so far in that you couldn't imagine your life without all that," his fingers formed imaginary quotation marks in the air, "power."

A low righteous growl filled the space between them. "This is not good, Necklim. I can't stand by and watch Katelyn fall to the same darkness Cara did."

Necklim patted his friend's shoulder. The frustration Nolan felt inside was transferred out through his words. "It doesn't end the same for them all, Nolan. You know that my friend." He turned to face him. "You also know, it's not up to us to decide which path a human chooses. That is their decision. We'll do all the Lord commands us to. That's all we can do. We'll remain on guard and ready at all times."

"Yes, I know. I will go and inform the others. We will be watching for your signal."

Necklim's heart ached for his fellow soldier in the Lord. "May your perfect peace surround him, Lord. Guide us through this."

He returned his focus back to their charge. "What's your plan, dear one?"

◆ ◆ ◆ ◆

Katelyn took comfort in the darkness of the woods that surrounded her. Hesitant to leave what little protection she thought she had, she turned and slowly stepped out from behind the tree. Determined, yet in no hurry, she started her journey to face the monster that had made her aunt's home its own.

She stopped at the edge of the drive. It was the only thing that stood between her and her destination. She took a deep breath and let it out. "Okay, here I go." The jagged gravel pressed deep into her already sore feet as she slowly placed her weight on them. She flinched, they were not as forgiving this time around.

After making her way up the steps and onto the porch, she stopped in front of the door. Her body stiffened. The hair on her arms rose as goose bumps covered her skin. *You can do this, Katelyn. You have to.*

Katelyn slowly pushed open the door, not knowing what she'd find on the other side. She stepped across the threshold and moved cautiously towards the stairwell. Standing with her back pressed up against the wall, she took one step at a time until she reached the second floor. *So far, so good. Now hurry up and get your stuff!* She stood at the entrance to the bedroom, reached around the door frame, and felt along the wall for the switch. The light flickered on, but brought no relief with it. She forced her shivering legs to carry her across the room. Without taking her eyes off the doorway, she knelt down beside the bed, pulled out her suitcase and flopped it open.

The clothes that hadn't made the floor their new resting place were tossed into the blue leather bound rectangle that awaited their arrival, leaving her with a big piled up mess, but she didn't care. Getting out of there was the only thing that concerned her. She picked up her phone and stuffed it into the soft-pocketed material of her shorts while slipping on her flip-flops, then stepped out of the room and looked around. She took in every little detail, sight, and sound before working up the courage to descend the stairs.

Katelyn reached out for her keys that were on the stand by the door, but kept her sight focused on her means of deliverance a few feet away. She wanted nothing more than to press the pedal to the floor and let the gravel fly.

Relief rushed over her as she opened the car door and threw the suitcase in the passenger side seat, then sat down, and locked the door. It was a false sense of security, she knew that.

She fought to steady her shaking hand and insert the key

into the ignition. After three tries she got it lined up and cranked it over. Nothing. Not the faintest sound.

"No! This isn't happening." She cranked it over again. Still there was nothing. "Oh, start already!"

She pounded the wheel with her fists in frustration. "Maybe I should just give up and let whatever is in that stupid house win!" She cringed at the words that angrily rolled off her tongue. She knew better. Her stubbornness wouldn't let her be overtaken so easily – would it?

"This has got to all be a dream. One crazy dream. None of it is real." She cursed under her breath. "I'm not cut out for this kind of creepy stuff." She took several deep breaths. "Oh, Aunt Cara. I wish you were here. Maybe you could explain all this to me. Wait a minute, is this what my mom tried to warn me about?"

A sudden movement on the porch told her she was no longer alone. *Great, just great.* She swallowed and fought hard against the urge to turn towards the house. Curiosity won in the end. A grotesque figure stood in front of the door, teeth exposed, claws ready to attack. It opened its mouth and released a loud shrill. Its body shook with laughter as long, dark wings spread out from behind it.

"No," she whispered. Fear filled every part of her body, leaving her motionless. "God, please help me!"

Ackmen stepped back at her words. Lips snarled. His chest rose and fell quickly. His yellow eyes bore into to her as feelings of unworthiness were whispered into her ear. She took the bait.

"I'm such a poor excuse for a human. I'm frail, weak, full of fear. What does that say about me?"

Her words cut to the very depth of her being. Were they true? She thought back over her life. The parties, drugs, one night stands, back talk, and disrespect of authority was just the start of a long list of mistakes she had previously made. "Even if there was a God, why would he help me? I'm a disgrace."

She sat silent for a moment trying to make sense of what she was seeing and feeling. "Wait a minute, what am I saying? Where's my stubbornness? I'm giving up too easily."

At once, a soft glowing light surrounded her. It was warm, and brought with it a peaceful feeling she couldn't explain. She gasped at the several glowing men-like beings that appeared in front of her clothed in armor, encircling the car. Their swords were drawn and pointed towards the starlit sky. Their eyes blazed with a soft golden fire.

"Angels?"

She stopped, her attention now focused on the one that stood directly in front of her. White, feathery wings unfolded from behind the fair-skinned angel.

Her mouth fell open. "They say seeing is believing, and yet —"

———◆◆◆◆———

"What are you doing here, Necklim," the demon hissed, "you have no claim here."

"I have claim to wherever the One who sits on the Mercy Seat says I have claim to Ackmen." Necklim replaced his sword in the sheath and focused his attention on the girl in the car. He spoke only one word to her spirit before they all disappeared. "Pray."

"Pray? What will that do for me? Prayer is something only Bible believers do, and I'm not a Bible believer. Okay, sure, I've heard of God and His angels, and Satan and his demons, and all that – wait if those were angels, then that means," she looked towards the house, "that means that is a demon?"

She shook her head. "Thanks to tonight, I don't know what I believe in anymore. A week ago, even a day ago I would have said the person had lost their mind who had seen such stuff! Now, here I sit in the middle of it all."

She thought back to her run-in with Miranda. "I guess what she has is the real deal?" She drummed her fingers on the steering wheel as she looked at the blue suitcase in the seat next to her. She leaned over, unzipped the front of it and reached into the tiny pocket where she had placed Miranda's card weeks before. She stared. Then slowly flipped it over and over again in her hand while contemplating sending a message. "Oh, why not? It's good to get a shock of a lifetime every once in a while. This is sure to be one for her. Me, Katelyn Burnsten, asking for prayer."

Nolan stood unseen next to the car door, looking down through the roof. That text would certainly help, but would it be enough? He would have to wait, only time would tell. The decision was hers. All the pieces were falling in place. "You can do it kid, just believe."

"Give her time, my friend."

"Time is something we don't have much of, Necklim." Nolan's voice was somber.

"We may not," Necklim pointed up to heaven, "but He does."

"We need to return to our posts."

"Yes, we do."

Necklim watched Nolan disappear into the night. He knew his friend's concern wasn't unfounded.

"Necklim," Ezera said, as he returned to his side with a report. "Your request has been granted. Prayer warriors are being awoken as we speak. One of the first was an old friend of Katelyn's."

"Yes, Katelyn sent her a text a little bit ago. We need to be more alert now. That will get Melti's and Latar's attention for sure. They will no doubt be joining up with Ackmen soon."

"Yes, I was afraid of that," Ezera replied.

"Ackmen isn't planning on giving up or losing any ground he may have gained." Necklim turned in Ezera's direction. "He'll have to call for help once the prayer covering gets in place. He's not going to like that."

"Will we need more warrior angels?"

"Yes. They'll be sent soon, very soon."

CHAPTER EIGHT

Ackmen paced the floor, trying to figure out where the massive-sized enemy soldiers had come from and how many of them there might be out there. Who was praying their interference into play? He had to find out. It had to be stopped.

He grabbed the living room curtain and moved it to the side, staring at Katelyn who had sat unmoved in the car for almost a half an hour. "At least those mettlesome angels have disappeared." His long pointed nail scratched the bottom of his chin. "Or have they? Why does that even worry me? They have no rule here. Who are they trying to fool anyway?" He flapped his wings behind him, then looked down at the spirit that was hovering near the floor. "You, go, find re-enforcements."

Ackmen let go of the curtain and made his way to what used to be Cara's bedroom. "Ah. This place always rejuvenates me." He picked up a brown book from the bed stand and thumbed through the pages.

"The very book that started the whole takeover of this family. How nice." His nails drummed against the cover of the book as he circled the bed. He stopped in front of the window and glanced at the car below. "Hmmm, I wonder." A sly smile parted his lips. "It never hurts to try."

He flew out the window and brought his body to an abrupt stop on the hood of Katelyn's small car, slightly denting in the sides under his weight. "You want answers, little one?" He tossed the book down and it thumped as it came in contact with the metal hood.

Katelyn swallowed hard. Ackmen never took his gaze off her as he slid the book out in front of him. "You'll find them in here, just as your sweet Aunt Cara did, and her mother Marie, and her mother Lizzie. Your family has long sought out our leader and his ways. Now it's your turn. You don't know how important you are." A hiss crept forth from his mouth.

Ackmen stepped off the hood of the car and ran his long gray claw down it, peeling the paint as it went. "Don't take too long. I'm not known for my patience."

Katelyn sat wide-eyed, her back glued to the seat. She wasn't sure what pure evil felt like – until then. The presence that filled the car and surrounded her had left no doubt in her mind that this was not something she wanted any part of.

A smothering sense of dread and sadness came over her. *Think of something fun, think of Trevor. Just think of something!*

Nothing worked. Second by passing second she become more enslaved to the fear that was squeezing every ounce of courage out of her.

"There's no use fighting me. You will not win." Ackmen's yellow eyes remained centered on her as he floated backward through the air. Only when he disappeared from her sight did the heavy cloud of emotions leave her.

She quickly looked back and forth from the door to her phone several times before finally keeping her eyes on the screen in front of her. She dialed her mom's number and waited.

"Hello?"

"Mom! Help me!"

"Katelyn what's wrong? Where are you?"

"I'm at Cara's still. I think I know what you were talking about concerning Aunt Cara."

"You've seen them then?"

"I've seen something, Mom. This thing is huge and it's scary. But I've also seen very tall man-like beings. They didn't scare me, though. They actually made me feel kind of peaceful. They spoke to the creepy things for a moment before turning to me and telling me to pray."

"Katelyn, there's still hope. Pray. They are angels. God has sent them to fight alongside you. Don't ignore their words. Don't show fear, don't be afraid. The demons feed off that."

"But Mom, I'm not saved. I don't even know if I believe in God."

"I know, Katelyn, but He believes in you."

"Mom?"

"I've been attending church. I've been learning a lot. Trust me, Katelyn. He wants you free of what's been passed down through your dad's family. I didn't believe it was true for a long time. But certain things that happened made me wonder."

"I don't want to be alone right now, Mom. My car won't start, and I'm not going back into that house. Should I leave?"

"No, I'm coming. Call Trevor, he's closer. The Lord will

fight for us tonight. We won't run."

"Please hurry."

"I will, Katelyn. I'm in my car now. Pray."

The click informed Katelyn of the disconnected call. She thought about Trevor. It was true that he was closer, but would he understand all this? "His parents are Christians," she reasoned.

Thoughts of her aunt being caught up in all of this nonsense distracted her. How was it possible to ignore the evidence before her on the hood? Conflict rose within her. Part of her wanted to know the truth, and part of her yearned for all this to be over.

She turned the key over again and pumped the gas pedal as fast as her leg would allow. "Come on! Lord, please let it start."

Nothing.

She gave up and a few minutes later dialed Trevor's number. "I can't stay here any longer."

"Hey, miss me already, huh?" Trevor's country accent filled her ear.

"Well, ya know. What can I say? What are you doing right now?" The deep inhaled breath before she spoke didn't hide the fear in her voice like she had hoped.

"Just watching some television before heading to bed. Why? What's wrong?

Hurry up, think of something.

"Oh, ummm, I was just wondering if you'd like to go out for a little bit. I need some things from the store, and I didn't want to go alone."

She knew her excuse was lame, but she couldn't risk telling him the truth to have him laugh it off and not come at all.

"It's a little late to be going to the store, but sure, I'll go with you. Let me get my shoes on and I'll be on my way."

"Great!"

Chill out. He's going to think you're crazy.

"I didn't know going to the store was so exciting."

"Well, you know, you had to drag me out of this place, and now, I just love to go."

"Oh, okay then. I'll be leaving in a few minutes."

"All right, see ya soon. Oh and, Trev, thanks."

"No problem."

She twirled the phone in her hand. "Just a few more minutes and I'll be out of here." She inhaled; the muggy, stale air filled her lungs. She looked towards the house and then back out in front of her. "Crap, the book. What am I suppose to do with that?"

She looked around the front seat but didn't see anything that would be of any help, so she turned towards the back. A multicolored umbrella lay off to the right hand side, next to the door. "Yes." She pushed her feet against the floor of the car and stretched out until she was able to reach it, then pulled it to her.

Her fingers trembled as she wrapped them around the knob of the handle. With each gradual turn the glass beside her disappeared a little more, widening the open gap between it and the frame. She kept her sights on the front door as she slid half her body out the window and lined the tip of the umbrella up with the edge of the book. She pulled the umbrella back and then shoved it forward as hard as she could. The book slid and landed with a thud on the gravel in front of the car.

She faced the house, unaware of the multitude of glowing yellow and green eyes that glared back at her from all different directions.

Wasting no time she returned inside the car and rolled up the window as fast as she could. Her efforts were brought to a stop by an invisible force.

"Leave me alone," she screamed.

"I can't do that. I've already told you, you are too important." The unseen demon laughed in her ear before returning back to the house, book in hand.

Chapter Nine

Miranda couldn't remember ever having such a strong call from the Lord to pray. Heaviness weighed on her like a boulder, making it hard to concentrate on her words. The text she received from Katelyn only confirmed and added to her unrest. She remained on bended knees, the urgency in her prayers increasing as a vision flooded the screen of her mind.

Hundreds of horrifying beings in different sizes stood in rows upon rows on the left hand side of an open field. Their curved swords were held out in front of them. Low growls could be heard throughout the ranks as they revealed their long, pointed teeth behind their snarled lips

She panned the sight in front of her again. A rundown house sat yards in front of the angry horde of demons. A young girl stood frozen with fear on the porch. Her shrill screams not only reached her ears, but they seemed to hype up the demons as well. It was as if each scream increased their restlessness and desire to attack. Something held them back, although she wasn't sure what. She glanced back and forth between the girl and the demons, as she whispered prayers through her quivering lips.

The crowd parted as each demon stepped aside and made way for an unseen force. She could feel its crushing presence and strained to see it, but the darkness kept it hidden until it finally stepped out in front of its enraged army.

A loud gasp escaped before she could cover her mouth. The large demon turned his head, his eyes red and empty bore into her. She quickly ducked down in the tall grass around her. Fear tried to grip her, but she prayed against it.

"Get her, Ackmen! We must stop her annoying prayers."

"Yes, Melti."

She heard them hiss to one another, but she continued to pray, ignoring the thunderous footsteps that came in her direction. They stopped inches from her bent body. She looked up into the eyes of the hideous figure that stood over her, but to her surprise he looked right through her.

"I don't see her," Ackmen said.

"You incompetent failure! Get back over here. It's almost time to claim her," Melti ordered.

Miranda opened her tear-filled eyes. What Katelyn was up against was much worse than she could have ever imagined. Almost an hour passed but there was still no relief, her spirit remained unsettled.

"Lord, I don't know what's going on, but no matter how long it takes, I'll remain in prayer for Katelyn. Please protect her, Father."

She made several phone calls requesting prayer before returning to her own.

Hushed whispers flowed from some hidden place within. A place she didn't know existed. Tears streamed down her reddened cheeks like a waterfall. She raised her hands towards heaven in adoration and worship of her Savior. Whatever was going on, she knew that He was the only one who could help.

———◆◆◆———

Latar passed back and forth across the rugged floor, his long nails scraped the walls leaving behind an indented streak. Thoughts of taking out his frustration on the heavenly army crossed the distorted waves of his mind. "They have no idea what awaits them tonight! How can they be so careless? Do they really think tonight will end well for them?"

Latar's lower ranking demons that always accompanied him, cowered in his presence. "Well?" His voice echoed off the walls.

"We don't know, sir," they replied in unison.

His eyes narrowed as pure hatred radiated from them. "I don't know either. But they will learn a hard lesson tonight."

"Latar, sir," a demon bowed, "Melti has arrived."

"Send him in."

Melti passed through the open archway, head held high. "Ackmen called for backup. It appears our enemy has arrived."

Latar stopped in front Melti and placed his crooked finger under his chin. Melti swatted it away. "Do not think to threaten me, Latar. I'm not some puny demon under your command. I'm your equal. Remember that. Besides, our enemy will not prevail."

"I know they won't. Katelyn is far more important to us than her aunt Cara ever dared to be. Cara was a pawn, a great one, but nothing more. These heavenly warriors must not get in our way, they need to be disposed of." Latar released his rage against the innocent cave walls. They shook as his constricted fist collided with them. The stone cracked, loosening tiny pebbles which fell to the ground.

"Let's go put an end to this mess," said Latar.

They left the cavern. Their flight into the night sky was quick and precise. They dove and maneuvered through the trees and tall buildings around them, unseen to the humans below that were carrying on with their everyday lives. Oblivious to the fight for each of their souls.

"I sense a battle tonight, Melti. A dangerous one."

"As do I, Latar. As do I."

Necklim had watched Katelyn slide the book off the car. He had given himself permission to smile, be it ever a slight one. Her refusal to Ackmen's invitations thus far, mixed with the prayer covering, were making a difference. Her strong will, in this case, was turning out to be a positive thing. Every minute he felt his strength increase and the territory towards the house grow. That was sure to gain more demons' attention. He sent out a signal to his fellow Warriors to be on alert, and then looked to the night sky. Only time would tell when the battle would begin, but he was ready.

His keen senses alerted him to the evil that resonated through the air. Melti was coming, and Latar was with him. Their overbearing figures were silhouetted in the light of the moon, still some distance away. His curiosity drew his attention in Ackmen's direction. He knew that if he felt their presence, Ackmen had felt it, too. He watched as a devious grin crept along the thin lines on Ackmen's face and gratification overtook his features.

Necklim concealed himself as the commanding demons lowered themselves to the ground. They huddled in a circle, surrounded by shadows and wisps of darkness, no doubt coming up with a plan of action. They may be evil, but when it came to a fight, they were definitely not naïve. Their wisdom showed forth in the strategies they executed during battle.

"I know you're here – Necklim. I can feel you. You will not win this battle. The girl is ours," hissed Latar.

Necklim waved his sword in the air, alerting his army. He could feel the time drawing near. He prayed for strength and knowledge for the upcoming battle as he made his way to the car that housed the very reason for his being there.

Questions, fear, and confusion were etched in the bunched up skin that set between her brows and in the two defined lines that crossed her forehead. His command was to let her know they were still there, and that's just what he planned to do. "Lord, let Your peace surround us all," he prayed.

"Katelyn," he whispered in a calm and peaceful voice. "We are here to help you. Don't be afraid. Pray."

She blinked several times before her lips moved. "We?" She could hardly get the words to come out of her mouth. "Pray?" She watched as Necklim moved his arm, and several angels appeared before her.

"These are Warriors, just like myself. We were sent here to help you."

"Sent here to help me, by whom?"

Necklim knew he had to be cautious with his words. He took a deep breath and let the glory flow from his body. "From God, Katelyn."

"God?" she questioned.

"Yes, God."

Katelyn closed her eyes and shook her head. Demons were real. She had had the not-so-great privilege of being aware of their existence. Angels were real, she had seen them, too. But God? God she hadn't seen. "Is God actually real?" she whispered to herself.

"God isn't something, or someone, that I've ever given much thought to," she said.

"I know," Necklim responded. "But He has given much thought to you."

"He has?" Katelyn looked at him questioningly. His smile brought a sense of comfort to her. "God has thought of me?"

"Yes, Katelyn."

"I don't know what to say to that."

"You don't have to say anything." Necklim again took a deep breath and sent up a silent prayer. "I do need you to listen though. We don't have much time. You have prayer warriors lifting you up before the Throne right now. You have us here with you. I need you to remember that. No matter what happens, you must remember that." He spoke with a gently sternness to make sure she caught the seriousness of his words before he continued. "Melti, Latar, and Ackmen are here for you too. They have plans for you, just as God does. But they are so different than the wonderful path God has laid out for you." He pointed towards the house and continued, "Their plans are to hurt you. To guide you into everything evil in this world. It will ultimately leave you filled with a dark emptiness. Nothing good will come of it."

Katelyn lowered her head. "I've been seeing, feeling something in that house ever since I moved in. I hadn't before." She looked up into Necklim's soft, yet concern-filled eyes. "Cara, did they kill Cara?"

Lord give me the right words. "Their plan was not completed concerning Cara."

"I don't understand."

"Our time is about up, Katelyn. Remember God's love for you."

"How can God love a wretched thing like me?"

"Oh, Katelyn. You are not wretched. You are precious in His sight. Feel His love as it comforts you. I must go now, but I won't be far."

"Wait, don't go."

Necklim turned to face her. "God's at work, Katelyn. Don't lose hope."

Katelyn sat engrossed as the angels that were once beside her disappeared. Her heartbeat had slowed back to its normal rate while they were there with her, but was now picking up the pace again. She rested her head on the back of her seat and looked up towards the sky, the ceiling blocking her view. A tear ran down her cheek. She wiped it away. "So, you love me? You care about me? You even sent angels to help me? Is this real? Is that true?" The questions kept coming, one after another, leaving no time for response. "People are praying for me?" Her thoughts went to Miranda. She looked down at the phone she had squeezed tightly in her hand.

A sudden heaviness blanketed her. The unseen spirit of doubt stuck its hook-like nail into her heart, and started to pluck out each small ray of hope that had just been planted there.

"That's enough." Necklim's sword poked the backside of the spirit's neck, bringing his message across loud and clear.

The spirit shrieked, then quickly composed himself. "Get your sword off me. You're standing on our ground, angel boy, or did you forget that?"

"I'm afraid you're mistaken. I am standing on the Lord's ground, and you are harassing someone the Lord sent me to protect. Or did you forget that?"

Katelyn couldn't explain the conflict going on inside her. She'd never known these feelings before. Hope, overpowered by doubt, overtaken again by hope. She could only imagine what was going on around her. Necklim's words were still fresh in her mind, "They are here for you too." Was there a battle going on about her right now?

CHAPTER TEN

Katelyn glanced at the clock on her phone before dialing her friend's number. *Twenty minutes sure does go by slow during a time like this. Where are you guys?*

She waited, anxious to hear her voice on the other end of line. It rang four times. She went to hang up, but something told her to wait for one more ring, so she did.

"Hello?"

"Miranda, it's Katelyn."

"Katelyn! Are you all right? I've been praying for you all night."

Katelyn wasn't sure how to answer Miranda's question. She didn't want her to think she was crazy. "No, I'm not. I've been through some strange things these last couple weeks."

Katelyn waited for Miranda to reply, but she didn't, so Katelyn went on. "I guess you could say my eyes have been opened. Anyway I was wondering if you would tell me about – about God."

"Yes, I can. What would you like to know?"

All of Katelyn's other inquiries would be based off Miranda's response to her first and foremost question, so that's where she started. "Is God, real? I mean really real?"

"What do you think about Him? Do you think He's real?"

She hadn't expected her former friend to reply the way she did. It was a simple yes or no question, or so she had thought. "Honestly, up until today, no I didn't believe in Him. I thought the whole idea of God, and His wondrous love was a joke. I thought people used Him as a crutch. As something to lean on to try and calm their own conscience, I guess."

"And now?"

"Now, now I'm starting to think He's real."

"He is real, Katelyn. He is very real. And so is His love for you. He thinks about you. He knows you."

"Yeah, so I've been told. I can't quite wrap my head around that, though. It's a strange concept to me."

"Who told you?"

"Miranda, I don't know if you'd believe me if I told you." Katelyn rethought her statement. "Well, maybe you would."

"I'm listening."

Katelyn cleared her throat. "Don't hang up on me."

"I won't."

"An angel told me."

"An angel."

"See, I knew you would think I was crazy."

"No, Katelyn, I don't think you're crazy. I think you are very blessed, loved, and guarded. I believe all His children are."

"But that's just it, Miranda, I'm not a child of God. I don't know much about how all that works, but I'm pretty sure I'm not God's child."

84

"That may be true, if you haven't accepted Jesus as your Savior, but you can be. You can be a child of God."

"But why would He send His angels when I'm not His child? Why would He want to protect me and look out for me even though I haven't accepted Jesus?"

"Because He's reaching out to you, Katelyn. And He's reaching out to you because He loves you."

"It's hard to believe that God would love me. You have no idea the things I've done in my life."

"You're right. I don't know. But He does, and He still loves you...in spite of it all. He sent His Son to a lost and dying world. Not to one that was perfect. We have all sinned. We all fall short of the glory of God. We all make mistakes. Yet, He still loves us. He still wants us to choose life."

"I find it hard to believe you've done anything wrong in your life, Miranda."

"Anything apart from God is sin. And even though I'm saved, Katelyn, it doesn't mean that I don't mess up."

"How, how does one accept Jesus?" Katelyn's voice was low. She fought against her own feelings, not sure if she really wanted to know. She waited for Miranda to answer but heard nothing.

"Miranda? Are you there?"

She pulled the phone away from ear and looked it over. An outline of an empty battery flashed in the upper left hand corner three times before the screen finally went black. "Great time for a dead battery."

Katelyn felt a presence next to her. She turned as a warm glow appeared through her window revealing the muscular man-like form next to her.

"Katelyn, you are not alone. We are here with you.

Remember that." Necklim's commanding, yet soft voice brought some relief to her to frazzled nerves.

"I'm glad you are with me. I don't know that I could have made it this far without you being here."

"You should know the battle will begin soon. We have a great number on our side already. More are standing ready if they are needed."

"There's a lot of them too, isn't there?"

"Yes, but you must remember, this isn't something new to us. We've been battling these fallen ones for a very long time."

Katelyn didn't respond. She took a moment and let the words of the armored angel beside her sink in. There were more. More evil, hideous, vile *things* yards from her, with stares that she was sure could turn her very soul to stone if they were able, and they were after her. Ready to fight for her. She couldn't help but shudder.

"What's your name?" she asked, unsure if she'd get an answer, or if in the end it mattered, but she longed to know anyway.

"My name is Necklim." He pointed to an angel that suddenly appeared on his right, "This is Nolan. And this," he nodded to his left, "is Sarta. There are many surrounding you and this land right now as I speak."

Katelyn nodded her head, her features etched with amazement.

Necklim smiled at her warmly. "Stay strong," he whispered before each of them faded from her sight.

She gripped her hands around the steering wheel. Miranda's words replaced the conjured up images of the demons in her mind. "He loves me? God himself, loves me? I don't know, Lord. It's taken me my whole life to finally open my mind and heart to believing in you. It seems after today's events, it would be foolish of me not to. How can everything I've seen and felt be real, and not You?"

Katelyn did her best to ignore the uncomfortable feeling that came upon her, to fight back against the thoughts that assaulted her, but she caved in her own strength. "So, this is the low I've sunken to? What will praying do for me, anyway?"

The spirit of despair grinned as she spoke out loud the suggested thoughts he'd place in her mind. She didn't know the power that her words held, but he did.

"Oh, forgive me for my unbelief, Lord. Help me."

A familiar voice whispered in her ear, cutting off the struggle she felt raging inside. "Those thoughts are not from the Father, Katelyn. Be careful not to speak the negative things being thrown at you. There's power in your words. Your enemy knows what makes you tick. He knows your weaknesses. He can tell how you feel by your reaction to his lies. He's been watching you for a long time, but your defender, your Savior, your God, should you choose to accept Him as such, has been watching you a whole lot longer."

Katelyn fought hard to keep Necklim's words from slipping away. She needed them to drive out the darkness that tried to rule over her. The peace they brought to her troubled soul was something she had coveted for such a long time. She tried to imagine what life would be like placing all her worries and stress into the hands of a God she'd never before believed to be true. The love that Miranda spoke of, that Necklim spoke of, could honestly be hers. The thought was humbling. She could feel the hard shell around her heart begin to chip away. It was odd. Strange. Scary. She had buried her true identity, keeping it sheltered for so long, that she wasn't sure she'd even recognize the girl inside.

Cara's smile crossed her mind, causing her to wonder if it was really sincere. How true to life her bubbly character was, or if it was a facade. Just a very well-played game of charades. Surely not all of her happiness was a mask. Everyone, though, hides their true colors sometimes – right? She thought back to her own mask, her own hiding, her own calloused heart. "My heart is hard, Lord. I have built up so many walls around it, and although I feel tiny chips of that stone being knocked away, I'm not sure You could break through all of them. I'm not sure I'm ready for them to be broken. I see a long road of stubborn rebellion ahead. I don't deserve Your love, or Your protection."

"Pray, Katelyn." Necklim's voice cut through her internal deliberation.

"Shut up you old fool," Latar yelled, a red foul mist spewed from his mouth with each word. "She knows she's not worth your God's love. You won't win her. You nor Nolan. You should stop trying while you're ahead."

Nolan's eyes narrowed as the radiance of God glowed around him. "Your words, Latar, have no affect on me."

"Is that right? Well, we'll see how little affect they have on you when you fail Katelyn – just as you failed Cara."

Necklim put his arm in front of his friend's chest, stopping him from going any farther. "It's not time, Nolan."

"Yeah, Nolan," Latar hissed, "it's not time. It's not yet time for you to watch her heart be pledged to our work. Besides, what does your *Commander* want with such a messed up girl, anyway?" Latar stepped in front of Necklim, standing mere inches from him. "This sexually immoral girl, this drunk. This waste of a life...what does He want with her?

Latar stood in front of Necklim, reeking of the pride in his heart. His red eyes glowed like that of a raging fire as he waited for his opponent's response.

Necklim met Latar's words with a solid blow to the midsection of his raven colored leathery form. Latar flew back and landed with such force against the porch that it shook the wood of the house it was connected to. He flew to his feet, fury evident on his face. "You, Necklim, will be sorry you were ever commanded to guard this human. I will personally make sure of that."

Necklim stood unmoved, his fellow Warriors by his side. "He'll come at her with her past mistakes. We must speak to her before the spirit of Doubt gets a hold on her.

"Katelyn," Nolan crouched down next to the car door, an urgent pleading in his voice. "Confess your sins to the Lord. All of them. All the hate, bitterness, parties, drugs...all of it. Confess it. There's nothing you've done that God doesn't already know about, for He's watched you from the day you were conceived. Let Him heal you, Katelyn, He's the only one who can."

Latar moved forward, his hands clenched. "Be quiet, Nolan."

"I only take orders from one, Latar and that's not you. You can tell me to be quiet all you want, but until God commands my silence, it won't happen."

A thunderous noise broke through the glare of their stares, drawing everyone's attention to the sky. "Ah, more of my servants have come."

Latar eyed his forces as they landed in a row in front of him. He was pleased with his growing army. He pointed his crocked finger in the direction of the first two demons in line. "You, I want you to go pay a special visit to Trevor. He'll be on his way over here, but you must stop him. He's a risk to our plan. Once we get Katelyn, he won't be a problem anymore. He'll follow her right to us."

"Yes, our lord," they replied in unison, and turned to make good on their given orders.

Latar focused his attention on the next four in line. "You," he pointed at them, "you four go pay a visit to Trevor's parents. They're enemies. Their prayers will only hinder our plan tonight. You must stop them. I don't want them to be a concern to us."

"Yes, our lord." They bowed and then turned to take flight.

Latar counted the number of strong ones left in his army. "Seven, hmmm. I need most of you here with me to guard our captive. Unfortunately, there's another nuisance we need to cut off tonight." Latar's glance stopped on a small red demon in the middle of the line. "Doubt, you, yes you. Go and fill Miranda's mind with questions and uncertainty. Cause her to wonder why she's even praying for a former friend, when all she did years ago was put her down for her faith. Stir the thoughts of pride into her heart."

"Yes, my lord."

"Oh and Doubt, you'd better not fail me."

"I won't, my lord." Doubt leaped into the air, quickly flapping his small wings in the direction of the individual that had been assigned to him.

"The rest of you, position yourselves around the car. Invoke fear. She'll be easy to break down. Don't give up, don't stop. It won't take too long. Oh, and watch out for our enemies. Don't be fooled; even though you can't see them, they're out there. At least four. They are mighty, but we will prevail."

Latar moved back towards the house, motioning for Melti and Ackmen to follow him. They closed the door behind them and began discussing the next phase of their plan. A sneer crept along each of their thin charcoal gray lips.

"It's perfect, Latar."

"You are in charge, Melti. Make it happen. She's almost here."

"Melti stormed through the door and leaped into the air. His tattered dark wings, with each powerful flap, lifted him higher and higher into the darkness.

He flew seamlessly through the air watching as the animals of the night scattered at his approaching presence. He could hear the faint hum of an engine off in the distance. He increased his speed and within moments caught the soft white glare of two beams cutting through the darkness before them.

"There you are."

He veered to the left, circling just above the tree tops, leaving the few leaves that hadn't let go of their life force just yet blowing in the breeze he'd left behind. He trailed the silver compact car for the next five minutes, giving it just enough time to be in clear view of the anxious girl that awaited its arrival, before making his move. When the time was right, he thrust himself through back window, coming to stop in the passenger side seat in full view of the driver.

His sudden appearance took Leah by surprise. She yanked the wheel to the right, noticing the advancing vehicle seconds too late.

Melti hovered above the scene, watching as metal collided with metal, leaving Leah pinned between the driver's side door and the grill of the truck. He saw the crimson flow from her head and around the piece of glass that was embedded just above her temple. "Looks like my work here is done."

Latar drummed his appendages against the windowsill, surveying the scene in front of him. A low wave of laughter crept from deep within and slithered out into the stillness around him. "Hopefully the others are having the same luck with putting a stop to Trevor as Melti just had with putting a stop to Leah. I do see victory ahead, Ackmen. I can smell it in the air."

"As do I."

A glimmer next to the mangled car caught his attention, and was followed by a blinding light in the tree line. "Yes, Necklim, I'm well aware that you're still out there. Watching and waiting. Slowly your strength and covering will dwindle." Latar curled back his lips, making sure his long sharp teeth were in clear view. "Then you'll have nothing, and we'll have won her."

CHAPTER ELEVEN

Miranda knelt beside her bed, her spirit in tune closely with the Lord. Denab stood guard over her, encouraging her and protecting her. Not that he would have needed a warning with the stakes as high as they were tonight, but he was thankful one had come nonetheless. He lifted his sword and held it over her head as he spread his wings to cover her, keeping her hidden from any enemy eye.

Doubt didn't need anyone to announce his presence. Denab felt him coming a mile away. He didn't move from his position.

"I know you're here. I can feel you. You won't win tonight. You might as well give up. I'll break through your cover and have her doubting before the hour's up." Doubt slowly crept towards her bed. His hideous laughter filled the angel's ears.

Denab knew Doubt's ways. He refused to fall for his tricks. He stayed put and sent a prayer to the Throne for the grace and strength to complete his mission and keep Miranda in prayer.

"Katelyn will be ours. Our leader needs her, and what he wants, he gets. Nothing and no one will stand in his way. What does your master want with her anyway? She's just a worthless human. And this girl you're hiding, what is she? One person praying won't be enough to shield Katelyn from the coming claim on her soul."

Denab kept his line of communication open with the Lord, ignoring the countless discouraging words that were meant not only for his ears, but for his charge's spirit as well. He remained focused and continued his prayers and praise, letting each one of Doubt's words bounce off the invisible field that surrounded him.

Trevor pulled up to the wreckage that was feet away from the drive he had intended to turn into, unaware of the demon and angels that surrounded it. He put his car in park and stepped out just as the rain began to grow heavier. He flipped the hood of his jacket up over his head and ran towards the debris in front of him while he called for help.

He looked in the driver side window of the truck. "Are you alright in there?"

"Yes," he heard the man say. "Check on those in the car."

Trevor ran around the busted up heap of silver metal and knocked on the window. He got no response. "Hey!" he yelled and knocked harder. Still nothing. He yanked several times on the door before it finally opened. A woman's limp body fell to the side, stopped only by the seat belt across her chest. He gasped and stared at the woman in front of him. "Leah," he whispered. He glanced up at the house that sat back off the road unsure if Katelyn knew. He felt her neck for a pulse and sighed in relief when he'd easily found one. "Leah, it's Trevor, can you hear me?"

His question was met with a hushed groan. "Help is on

the way, Leah. Everything's going to be okay. Just hang in there."

His phone vibrated in his hand and he glanced at the screen, worried it was Katelyn. It wasn't.

"Hello, Mom. I'm kind of busy. Can I call you back?"

"Trevor, something's wrong."

"What, what's going on? Are you are all right? Is Dad all right?"

"We're fine, Trevor. It's Katelyn I'm worried about."

"Why, does she know about her mom's accident? I'm in front of Cara's house but I don't see any sign of her."

"No, Trevor. I haven't talked to her. Something's just not right, I can feel it."

Trevor wasn't into the whole religious thing. He just couldn't make himself believe that there was some other force behind all the happenings in the world. He had too many questions that didn't have answers. Yet he couldn't deny the fact that his mom's "feelings" were right pretty much every single time. He had witnessed it far too often growing up. So when his mom said she was concerned or worried about something or someone, he knew to pay attention.

He tried to shake off the dread that had started to take root.

"Mom?" Trevor's voice was shaky.

"Go to her, Trevor. She's going to need you. I'll call you later. I have to go. I have to cover you in prayer."

Trevor hung up the phone, a fearful look taking over his expressions. He wanted to run up the drive, but he knew he couldn't leave Leah. Not yet. Not until he could at least hear the sirens. He dialed Katelyn's number. Hearing her voice would put his mind at ease. He needed that. Several rings later and he was listening to her 'sorry I missed your call' message.

He hung up, then dialed his parents' number. "Dad, I'm in front of Cara's, Katelyn's mom was in an accident. I can't leave her. I tried calling Katelyn but she's not answering. The house is dark. I'm worried."

"I'm on my way, Trevor."

Trevor hung up and redialed Katelyn's number. Still there was no answer. "Everything's fine. She's probably just in the shower or something," he tried to convince himself. But it didn't work. His breathing only intensified. He closed his eyes as he slid his fingers through his hair. Worry was written in the lines of his face. He focused on keeping Leah as awake as he could. "Hurry, Dad, please hurry."

The squeal of tires against the wet pavement drew Katelyn's focused attention from the house towards the road several yards away. Two trucks and one small car were blocking the road. "Mom?" She went to open her door and froze remembering the unseen spirits. Giving herself a few seconds to think things over she grabbed the handle. Her mom was more important.

"You must stay here, Katelyn." Necklim stood in front of the door.

"What? I think that's my mom down there, and Trevor. I need to see if they are okay."

"You must trust me, your mom will be fine. Trevor will be up here shortly. He's waiting for the ambulance."

"So, it was my mom? What happened?"

"Katelyn, there's not much time. The attack has begun. You must choose."

Katelyn pulled her knees to her chest and held onto them tightly. She steadied her breathing and thought back on the words that Necklim had spoken to her. *I must be of some importance for all this to be happening to me. Right?* She longed to hear Necklim's confirmation, but there was only her voice running through her thoughts. *I'm worth something to God. I'm worth something to God. I am worth something to God.*

"Speak those words out loud. Speak truth into yourself." Necklim prompted her, but remained concealed.

Out loud? Truth? Even in her head those words seemed to lift her spirit a bit. *Why not? Okay, here it goes. I may sound crazy, but right now I don't care.*

She inhaled, closed her eyes, and whispered, "I'm worth something to God."

"Say it again. Louder." She heard Necklim's voice, but still couldn't see him.

"I'm worth something to God. I'm worth something to God. I am worth something to God." She kept repeating the words, louder and louder. Each time her belief grew. She knew what she had to do. What she'd been called to do.

"Dear God. I believe in you. I believe that you love me, and that you have a plan for me. Please forgive me for the wrongs I've done in my life. Set me free, and see me through this. Give me the strength to face and deal with what's before me tonight. I accept you, Jesus, as Lord, and Savior over my life."

The demons' displeasure pierced her ears and they revealed themselves. She swallowed the fear that tried to creep up her throat and out her mouth.

"You'll be sorry," Latar hissed, pointing in her direction.

A warm, bright light appeared and the demons fled. Katelyn looked out the side window and smiled at the glowing angel that stood next to her, and soaked in the peace that he brought.

"Keep praying, Katelyn."

Several angels landed in the front yard. Some took over guarding Katelyn while others joined with Necklim and Nolan. With confidence, they stood face to face with their enemies. One by one they pulled their shimmering swords from their sheaths and held them out in front of them. The glory of God shone around them and it caused the demons to raise their arms and spread out their wings in front of their faces.

"Well, well," Melti growled. He lowered his arm and looked Nolan up and down. "If it isn't my favorite defeated angel. I would have thought you'd been put on leave, you know, with your recent failure and all."

"Ignore him, Nolan. Stay focused," Necklim encouraged.

"Oh sure, he'll stay focused, won't you, Nolan," Melti mocked.

Nolan never uttered a response, instead he prayed to his Commander, and asked for a clear mind to be able to fight the battle he knew was only moments away.

"Line up and get ready, boys. I think we're about to have some fun," said Melti.

The demons took their stance behind their leader, swords drawn. Evilness filled every nook and cranny of their being. Hisses and snorts escaped through their crooked grins. Their eyes glowed red and yellow. They twitched with excitement as they impatiently awaited the command.

"Are you sure you want to do this, Necklim?" Latar

turned and pointed to the army behind him. "It's quite obvious you're out numbered. Besides, the girl, how important is she really? In the grand scheme of things she's just one lowly, frail, pathetic human. There are so many others out there for you to watch over and protect. Why not just hand her over to me? We can end all this right now. No blood needs to be shed."

"Who says we're outnumbered? Our Commander never sends us to battle with less than we need."

Latar turned about, searching every inch of the sky and landscape. "You're lying," he growled.

"I'm an angel of the Lord, Latar. I do not lie. I have no use nor the time for lies. As far as Katelyn, she is not a pathetic human. She was created in the image of God, and is loved beyond measure. She is important to Him, and she is important to us. I will not hand her over to you, as I don't have the power to do so. That lies within her. She makes her own decisions. And the most important one that she'll ever make has already been made."

"You have ruined everything. You and your Creator. She was in our hands."

"Yet you let her slip through." Necklim titled his head, his sideways grin directed at Latar.

"I won't ever make that mistake again." Latar glared and exhaled the red tinged smoke from his mouth.

"We shall see."

Necklim remained motionless listening for the command from his Leader before reacting to the head demon's threat. He didn't have to wait long. A whispered voice spoke to his heart through the mist of the commotion. "Now, Necklim. Now."

He gave the nod to his fellow angels and they flew into

the air. His white feathery wings carried him up and over Latar. A brilliant light streaked through the dark sky as he swung his sword in Latar's direction. Latar reached up and grabbed it, stopping it only inches from his face and shoving it back, giving him just enough time to grab his own sharply curved sword. Latar sent it flying through the air. A loud clang rang out as it struck the front of Necklim's breastplate, then fell to the ground.

"Nice shot. Now it's my turn." Necklim tucked in his wings and barreled toward Latar with lightning speed, knocking him off his feet and back onto the porch. Necklim was on top of him, the tip of his sword beneath Latar's chin before he even knew what hit him. "Look around you, deceiver. Tell me now, what do you see?"

Without moving his head Latar took in the spiritual war that raged on in front of him. One swipe of the angel's sword and the demon they were engaged with was defeated. "More will come. You will see. You will not win," Latar responded.

"Look up, Latar. Tell me, what do you see?"

Latar removed his focus off his defeated army and looked up. Thousands of angels filled the sky. Each shone brightly against the darkness behind them. A rumble echoed from deep within him as he stared back at Necklim with narrowed eyes.

"More may come, Latar, but we are ready." Necklim spoke the truth.

Trevor heard the sirens off in the distance. "Leah, help will be here soon. I need to go find Katelyn now."

"Protect her, Trevor," she sputtered.

"I will."

Trevor ran to his truck, jumped in and stuck it in reverse, then pulled in the drive, sending the gray gravel flying from his tires.

"Katelyn!" he yelled as he jumped out of the truck leaving the door open behind him.

"I'm over here, Trevor," she said and waved her hand out the window.

CHAPTER TWELVE

Latar pushed Necklim's sword off of his neck and stood up. "I will not admit defeat. This will not be finished until there's no life left in me."

"I can arrange that."

"You know, I usually leave the fighting for the others, but it seems my army is dwindling quickly. In which case, I will fight. I'll always fight, when it's worth it." He pointed his long sharp talon in Katelyn's direction. "And she's worth it."

"I must say I agree with you about that. Katelyn is worth it. I will fight until my death protecting her, and so will the rest of us."

Latar waved his bony appendages in the air. "Death...such a price to pay for a mere human, wouldn't you say? Ah, it seems we have company. Trevor's Bible-believing father. Wonderful. It seems nothing is going as planned tonight."

Necklim nodded towards the vehicle and several angels met up with the others. They surrounded Trevor's father as he exited the truck, and made his way over to where his son was.

The tension grew between Latar and Necklim. "Leave him be, Latar."

"I'm afraid I can't do that."

Necklim stood face to face with Latar. "I'm afraid that wasn't a request."

Latar grinned as the angels encompassed him, covering him from every direction. "You will need a lot more than this to hold me back," he laughed.

"That can be accomplished." With a single wave of his forefinger Necklim gave the command, and more angels surrounded Latar.

Trevor opened the door. He grabbed Katelyn's hand and helped her from the car. "What's going on? Are you okay?"

She looked past Trevor at his father standing behind him. He was intently watching a scene in front of him, lips moving. She figured he was praying.

"Katelyn?"

"Can you see them, too?"

"See who?"

"Nevermind." She tightened her grip around his hand. "We need to get out of here."

"Wait, Katelyn." She stopped at the strong hand on her shoulder. "You must stay here and fight," urged Nolan.

"Fight? How?"

"Katelyn, who are you talking to?"

"He can't see you, how do I explain all this?" Her weary eyes looked into the confident golden ones staring back at her.

"He needs to trust you. Just tell him the truth. Tell him what you see. You must hurry, though. We'll need prayer cover."

"Just tell him?"

Nolan cupped her face in his hands. "He'll believe you."

"Okay."

Trevor's look of confusion made her have her doubts about how easy this was going to be, but she had to try. And quickly. "Trevor, I don't even know where to start with all this or if you're going to believe what it is I'm about to tell you. But you must try to. Please?"

Trevor tilted his head. "I'll try, Katelyn."

"There are angels and demons all around us right now. They have been fighting. And I'm afraid, it's not over yet. Nolan told me I have to stay. I have to pray."

"Wait, who's Nolan? Why do you have to stay? Why are they fighting?"

"Nolan is one of the Warrior angels. I have to stay because they need my prayers." The next question she didn't want to answer. She knew once he found out it would be a struggle to get him to let her stay.

"Why are they fighting, Katelyn?"

She took a deep breath before answering. "They are fighting – over me."

"Over you? Why? No, you know what, never mind. I don't know what's going on, or why you're acting so strange but I'm getting you out of here." He turned to go, her hand in his.

"Trevor, I can't go. I wish you could understand." She pulled her hand away.

"Katelyn, it's almost time."

She nodded toward Nolan. "Okay."

"I must pray, Trevor. I understand if you need to go."

"I'm not leaving you."

Katelyn knelt down in the cool, wet grass. She tilted her head towards the sky, ignoring the raindrops that pelted her face, and began to pray. "Heavenly Father...."

Trevor watched, dumbfound. Since when did she believe in God? His heart churned. Memories of him attending Sunday school, VBS, and church services when he was younger all collided in his thoughts. Scriptures, long forgotten, formed on his lips. He shook his head, then looked up.

"If it's all real, if You are real, give me the courage and understanding to see what is around us right now." He slowly opened his eyes, terrified, but thrilled at what he might see. Nothing.

"What's wrong?"

The unexpected sound of his dad's voice startled him. "I can't see them, Dad. I can't see them."

When his dad remained silent, he looked towards him. "I guess you can, right?"

His dad placed his hand on Trevor's shoulder. "Not everyone is meant to see these things, Trevor."

"But why? Why doesn't God want me to see?"

"He has his reasons. You just have to trust Him."

"Trust, yeah, trust in something I can't see. Makes a lot of sense."

"Just because you can see something, doesn't mean you should necessarily trust in it."

"Yeah, I suppose you're right, Dad."

Tim patted Trevor on the shoulder. "You don't sound so convinced. One day, Trev. One day it will all make sense."

Trevor watched his dad kneel down beside Katelyn and

take her hand. He mulled over his dad's words. There was wisdom in them, but he wasn't sure he was ready to accept it yet. He wondered if he should be scared. Knowing unseen spirits, unseen to him anyway, were everywhere around them didn't set him at ease. Yet his dad and girlfriend were kneeling beside him on the ground. Their whispered words floated up into the air and their faces shone forth peace, mixed with determination.

"Trevor."

He looked at Katelyn and smiled. "Yeah."

"Come sit between us, will you?"

"Between you?"

She patted the grass, "Yeah, right here. Please."

A strange feeling surged throughout his body as he placed both feet where Katelyn's hand once was and lowered his body into an Indian style composure.

"Thank you."

The touch of her skin against his had never made him feel so alive before. He forced a grin.

"Now take your dad's hand." The urgency in her voice revealed the seriousness of the situation. He took his dad's hand. "Now what?"

"Now, we pray for you."

"For me?"

"Yes," she said as she nodded in his dad's direction. "Ready?"

Trevor felt a wave of warmth wash over them as their prayers grew in intensity. He wanted to run, to escape from the unfamiliar confines, but something was holding them in place, securing them, covering them, even though he could not see it, he could feel.

Latar bent down before Necklim as if in defeat, and waited for just the right moment to strike. He rehearsed in his mind the exact movements over and over again, so when the time came he'd be ready. He couldn't afford to miss. He didn't have to wait long. As Necklim stepped forward, Latar slid his wrinkled hand around his bent waist and grabbed on to the sword that hung from his side. His sinister grin was hidden by his bowed head.

"Necklim, wait, his hand – it's on his sword," Nolan cautioned.

Necklim peered through Latar's arms in the direction Nolan was pointing. "You're right, my friend."

Latar groaned in frustration. Just one more step and Necklim would have been history. There was no more time to waste, a little farther away than planned couldn't be that much different. He pulled the sword from its case and swirled it over his head, scattering the angels around him. A split second was all he had to accomplish his task. Necklim would have to wait. He spread his immense wings and leaped in Trevor's direction.

Nolan stretched out his wings adding to the coverage of the ones on the ground. He gritted his teeth, tensed his glowing form, and waited for the impact he knew was quick in coming.

Instead the familiar sound of metal on metal rang out just above his head. He remained unmoved at the sounds of the battle raging above him, and waited for his orders.

"Necklim, you are a thorn in my side," Latar fumed as he sliced the air with his sword, coming inches from his target.

Latar steadied his breathing and held the tip of his chosen weapon in his hand. He cocked his head, grinned, then sent it flying through the air. "I will not miss this time."

Necklim moved, but not fast enough. A sharp blade cut through the skin of his thigh, catching him off guard. He winced. It was in deep.

"I told you I wouldn't miss, Necklim," Latar said as he landed in front of him. "I know which strategy you will put into play and who you'll command to do what." He folded in his wings and took the three steps to where his targets were. "So, do you really think you will win this battle?" he said, not bothering to give another glance in his enemy's direction.

"I don't think we'll win this battle, Latar. I know."

"Oh, and how's that?" Latar turned, surprised to see Necklim right behind him.

"Now, Nolan!" Necklim shouted as he plunged his blade into the dark, thick chest of the demon in front of him. Nolan rose, drew his sword and sliced the monstrous head demon in two. Red gas filled the predawn sky as it floated up into the air.

All the angels stood and stared at the several demons that Latar had left behind. Screeches and obscenities filled the last bit of fading darkness as they leaped into the heavens.

"It's over, Katelyn," a soft voice spoke to her. "You and your friends are safe."

She opened her eyes and released Trevor's hand as she stood to face Necklim. "Saying thank you doesn't seem like enough for what you've done here tonight."

He smiled. "We all can feel your gratitude. It comes

through our Creator. We know how thankful you are, Katelyn."

"Does this mean it's over for good?"

Necklim wished he could answer yes, without any doubt, but he couldn't. He didn't know. "It's over for now. We don't know what the future holds, only the Creator does. I can promise you this though. If we're needed again, we will be here."

"That's good news."

"The Creator is with you always, Katelyn. Even if we aren't. He's your protection. Your guidance. Your rock. Lean on and trust in Him, and no matter what happens, you'll be all right."

"Yes, I know that now." She was quiet for a moment before she looked back in to the brown eyes of the Warrior angel standing in front of her. "Do you know what happened to my Aunt Cara?"

Necklim took a deep breath and placed his hand on her shoulder. "I believe deep down you already know the answer to that."

"I suppose I do. I wouldn't have believed it before, ya know, that she could do something like that. But I guess it makes more sense now. Fear and torment can do things to people."

"Yes, that's true. The Creator will bring comfort to you. You just have to let Him."

"Comfort, peace, it all sounds so nice. Especially right now."

"We must go now," Necklim said, giving her a reassuring smile.

"I understand. Will I see you again someday? Hopefully

under different circumstances," she sighed.

"Perhaps. Farewell, Katelyn. Be strong. Stand on His word."

"I will."

Necklim signaled the other angels. Their swords met in the air. "For the Worthy!"

A bright blue and white light streaked through the morning sky as she waved goodbye to the angels that had so fiercely and faithfully watched over her and fought for her through the night. "Until next time," she whispered.

"Katelyn?"

She turned.

"Angels?" Trevor questioned as he pointed upwards.

She laughed, "Yes, angels."

"So they left?"

"Yes."

"Does that mean this is over?"

"That means this battle is over. Only God knows the future. Either way, as long as He's on my side, I know I can face anything."

Trevor wrapped his arms around her waist and gently pulled her close. "And what about me? Do I get to face the future with you?"

"That all depends." She smiled and laid her head on his chest.

"Depends? Depends on what?"

"Do you want to?"

He leaned back, slipped his finger under her chin, and titled her head up towards him. "I do. But we have a lot to talk about. You have so much to explain to me about what happened here."

"It wasn't just last night," she sighed. "But I will tell you all about it later. I promise. Right now I want some time to myself for a while."

"Oh, no, I'm not leaving you."

"You don't have to leave, Trev. You can stay downstairs. Maybe whip me up something to eat?" She asked innocently.

"That I can do."

"Great."

"Trevor," his dad called out. "Are you two going to be okay here?"

"I think we'll be okay, Dad."

Tim focused on Katelyn.

She shook her head yes. "I'm going to lay down for a bit, maybe. I would like for you and Mrs. Holcomb to come back later this evening, if you don't mind. I'm sure I'll have a lot questions once I'm able to get my thoughts sorted out."

"We'd love to. We'll see you both around five?" he questioned.

"Five sounds perfect," she smiled.

"Dad, thanks for coming. It means a lot."

"That's what family is for." He smiled and nodded in Katelyn's direction. "Call if you need anything."

"Thank you, Mr. Holcomb."

"Please, call me Tim."

Katelyn and Trevor wrapped their arms around each other as they watched his dad pull out of the drive. They stayed motionless until the truck was out of sight.

"Well, shall we go inside?"

"Yes." She took his hand and wove her fingers snuggly

between his. "I need to know how my mom is. Will you take me to the hospital after I freshen up?"

Trevor lifted her hand to his mouth and kissed it gently. "Of course I will. You know they would've called if something was serious."

"My phone's dead."

"Oh, that would explain why you never answered."

"Necklim told me she'd be okay. I trust him."

"Well, then, I'm sure she's just fine."

Katelyn smiled, then headed upstairs. Once the door was closed behind her, she freely let sobs that she'd been holding back for so long have full control. Her chest heaved, her body shook. The release felt like purifying water over her wounded soul.

CHAPTER THIRTEEN

Necklim and his fellow Warrior angels knelt before their Commander in the Throne Room. Their hands rested on their knees, heads bowed.

"Necklim, Sarta, Denab, Nolan." They rose, one at a time at the sound of their name. "You've each done good and completed your missions. Katelyn is safe for now."

"For now?" Nolan asked.

The Commander let a slight smile cross his lips. "Yes, my Warrior. For now." He glanced over each one before he continued. "You know the enemy will not give up so easily. There's still a plan in place for her family line. But not only has evil been made known to her, the goodness has as well."

Nolan nodded his head, "You speak the truth, as always, Commander."

"I'll be sending Guardians down to watch over Katelyn, her mom, Trevor, his family, and Miranda as well. They will be targeted more."

"Shall you need us again, it would be an honor to protect and fight for Katelyn and her friends. Anytime."

"I would like for you to meet the Guardians I've assigned to them." He called out their names, "Nove, Asleri, Makoi,

Basholi, Kanone." The Guardians entered the room one at a time and knelt before the One on the Throne, then nodded in the Warriors direction.

"Guardians," the Commander waved His hand towards the four angels that had stepped to the side, "these are the Warriors that were just released from your current charges. They fought hard to keep their souls from harm. Now it's your turn to fight just as hard to protect them."

"Yes, Commander," They stated in unison.

"Kanone, you will guard Katelyn. Nove, you will guard Trevor. Basholi, you will guard Miranda. Asleri, you will guard Trevor's parents, and Makoi, you will guard Leah, Katelyn's mom."

"Yes, Commander."

"Go now to your charges. Be watchful."

Necklim, Nolan, Sarta and Denab observed the Guardians as they flew from the Throne room to their new positions on earth.

"They will be well guarded, Nolan."

"I know, Commander."

"Let's give Nolan a moment," Necklim said.

"That's a wise idea, Necklim," the Commander replied in a gentle voice.

"Nolan."

He turned back towards the Commander after the doors to the room shut behind his fellow fighters."

"Yes, Commander."

"Nolan, tell me what's on your mind."

"Forgive me, my Lord. But I'm positive you already know that."

"True. I want to hear it from you, though."

Nolan sighed. "I'm concerned for Katelyn."

"Why? Do you not trust the light that's been started in her life?"

"It's not that, my Lord."

"What is it then, Nolan?"

"The book, Commander. It's been in her family for a long time. It has had a strong impact in past generations."

"That's true, Nolan. Katelyn now has something she didn't have before though – the knowledge to fight against that evil force. To break that for not only herself, but future generations as well. Correct?"

"Correct, my Lord."

"Trust the Guardians to do their work, Nolan. They will call on Me if help is needed. In return, I'll summon you and the others."

"Yes, Commander."

"Go now and rest."

Nolan nodded and slowly made his way through the heavy door that separated him from the paradise on the other side of it. The beauty in front of him grabbed his attention like it never had before. Letting out a sigh, he stretched his massive wings out behind him, then took off in the direction of his own little slice of heaven.

Miranda slowed the car and pulled to a stop just in front of Cara's house. An emotional prayer filled night had finally ended and she felt the burden lift just as the small rays of sunlight peeked through her curtains. Her heart had lifted, her spirit was full of peace. All had been worked out for His glory.

She stepped out of the car and closed the door. Trevor met her on the porch, cup of freshly made coffee in hand.

"How is she?" Miranda asked.

"Surprisingly, she seems okay for what she went through last night."

"She'd sent a text asking for prayer, then called later with some questions about God. I thought I'd stop by before church and check on her. Do you know what happened?"

"Honestly, Miranda, I don't know where to start, what to say, or if you'll even believe me. It's a bit much for me to take in and understand. I'm not sure I'd be the best person to tell you what happened here last night."

Miranda glanced back at the car and then leaned in a little closer. She traced her finger around the dent, and followed the scratches to the grill. "She saw them. That poor girl must have been scared to death."

"Saw them?"

"Demons. She had a confrontation with demons. Didn't she?"

Trevor shook his head slowly. "So you know about all that stuff?"

"Yeah, I do."

"Maybe the story won't seem as strange to you then."

"Did you see them too?"

"No. I don't think I'd want to."

"Don't feel bad." She patted his shoulder. "I wouldn't want to either."

"It wasn't just demons she saw. There were angels too. She talked to them. I thought she was going crazy or something. Talking to thin air."

"Understandable," she smiled.

"She was at peace though, towards the end of all the commotion. I could tell there was something different about her."

"Oh yeah?"

"Yeah."

"I don't know how she kept going, knowing those *things* were around, and worrying about her mom."

"Her mom?"

"Yeah, she was in a car wreck right there," Trevor pointed to the section of road that had displayed the collision front and center hours before.

"Wow, is she okay?"

"I think so. We're going to go see her after she freshens up."

Trevor didn't offer up any more information, so she didn't push him. He might not have seen the things going on around him with his own eyes, but she was sure he had seen the fear and confusion through Katelyn's. Miranda glanced at her watch. "I'd best be going or I'm going to be late. Will you tell Katelyn I stopped by?"

"Sure."

"Thanks. If it's all right, I'd like to come back by after church."

"Sounds fine to me, not sure if she'll be up to it though."

"Have her call me later, anytime after one will be okay."

"Wait, what's your number? Her phone's dead." Trevor grabbed the black rectangular object from his pocket and handed it to Miranda. She typed in her name and number before handing it back to him.

"Talk to you soon, Trevor."

"Bye."

Miranda glanced back and forth between the drive and the rear-view mirror as she drove away, praying for their protection and peace. "Dear Lord, what did the enemy have in store for her last night?" She shook her head. "No matter. Whatever it was you put a stop to it. Thank you."

Katelyn sat quietly in the blue cushioned chair next to her mom's hospital bed. The small, white, square taped above her temple was smudged with a red line. The machines fought off the quiet solitude with their constant beeps. Katelyn couldn't take anymore. She picked up the remote that was lying next to her mom's side and pushed the TV button. She flipped through channels, stopping on one that had a man dressed in a nice suit standing on a carpeted platform in front of a bunch of people. She held down the volume until she could hear the man's voice.

"Katelyn, is that you?"

She turned to see her mother squinting in her direction. "Yes, Mom. I'm sorry, I didn't mean to wake you."

"You didn't."

"How are you feeling this morning?"

"Probably better than I look," she grinned.

"You don't look bad, Mom. You actually look better than I imagined you would."

"Ah, yes, you do have an active imagination."

"Yes, I do." Katelyn turned off the TV and picked up her mom's hand, tracing the deep lines across her knuckles. It was the first time she'd looked at her mom's hands so intently since she was a child. Years of working, cleaning, cooking and like were starting to take their toll, erasing the youthfulness they once had. She sighed.

"How did things turn out last night?" her mother whispered.

"Well, I think they turned out for the best. I see things a lot more clearly now. And I've given my life to the Lord."

The pressure increased around her hand as her mom squeezed it, "Oh, Katelyn. I'm so glad to hear that."

"I thought you might be."

"Trevor's parents are stopping by after church, along with Miranda."

"That's good. They can talk to you, help teach you things."

"So can you. Last I heard you've been attending church, too."

"Yes, that's true. And I will talk with you. I want to hear all about what happened. But right now, I think I need some more rest."

"I promise to tell you everything when you get better and get out of here."

"Good."

"I'll also take that as my cue to go, too." She leaned down and kissed her mom on the forehead. "I'll be back to see you tomorrow. I love you, Mom."

"I love you too, Katelyn."

CHAPTER FOURTEEN

Katelyn sat across from Trevor at the kitchen table. The idea of meeting up with Miranda had taken over her thoughts. Could it really be that easy? The ending to their once strong friendship wasn't on the best of terms. How would things play out after all this time?

Trevor cleared his throat and brought her back to the present. "Everything okay?" he asked.

She focused her attention from the tiny blue-flowered pattern of the kitchen wallpaper to the man she had fallen in love with. "Yeah," she smiled. "Just trying to decide what to do about this evening."

"I see."

"What do you think? Should we have her stop by?"

Trevor set his cup of water down before he answered. "Honestly, I think it would be a good idea. Miranda's a Christian," he reasoned.

"Yes."

"Well, I'm thinking she probably knows a lot more about this stuff than we do, ya know?"

"I suppose." She thought for a moment. "I'm one lucky lady, you know that? To have you in my life. I really believe that any other guy would've gone running and never looked back after what happened last night. Can't say I'd blame him, though. It was crazy, to say the least."

"Yep, that's for sure. You're stuck with me though, like it or not."

"Promise?"

"I promise."

Katelyn looked at the clock. The hours had passed quickly, too quickly. "I guess I'd better make that call," she held out her hand. "Mind if I use your phone?"

"Not one bit."

She tapped her fingers against the table as she listened to the recording that greeted her. In a way, she was relieved Miranda didn't answer. Not that talking with her would have been bad, she just wasn't sure what to say. At least the greeting gave her a couple more seconds to pull her thoughts together. "Umm, hi, Miranda. You can stop by tonight around five if you're not busy. Trevor's parents will be here as well. Okay, so, I guess we'll see you soon then. Bye."

"Are you nervous?"

"Yes, a little. It's been a long time since I've talked with Miranda."

"It seems certain things have a way of working themselves out."

"Funny, Trev. It's not you in the hot seat right now."

"Sure it is."

Katelyn gave him a question look, "Oh, how so?"

"The way I see it, if you're in the hot seat, then so am I."

"Well," she stood to her feet and straightened her shoulders. "I suppose we'll have to come back to this – maybe. Our guests will be here shortly and I have to figure out something to feed them."

"Oh, Dad said he was going to pick something up. I talked with him while you were visiting with your mom."

"That's sweet of them." Katelyn smiled. She'd never see Trevor's parents in the same way again. The courage his dad had shown the night before would forever be etched in her memory. He didn't have to stay. It wasn't his battle or his very existence they were after. It was hers. And yet he chose not just to stay, but to fight.

"Trev, your dad's a good man. I'm sorry it's taken me so long to really figure that out."

"Yeah, you're right, he is. Don't feel bad, though. It took me a while to figure it out too, and I've lived with him my whole life."

Katelyn shook her head. "There's hope that my family will be that close, too, one day."

"Don't just hope, pray."

"Pray," she whispered. "That's what I'm going to do."

"Good, me too." He kissed her forehead.

"You too?"

"I've been thinking a lot about my life since last night."

"That's good."

Trevor shook his head as a smile crept across his lips. "How'd I ever get so lucky?"

"Luck had nothing to do with it."

She knew that now.

Trevor's parents arrived shortly after Miranda, bags of food in tow. "I hope everyone's hungry," Tim said, setting the bags down on the coffee table.

"I know I am," Katelyn said as she helped set out the food.

"We didn't know what everyone liked, so we just bought some cheeseburgers and fries. I hope that's all right with everyone."

"That's perfect."

"I'm sorry you guys. Where are my manners? Miranda, this is Mr. and Mrs. Holcomb, Trevor's parents. Mr. and Mrs. Holcomb this is..." Katelyn stopped, she wasn't sure how to introduce Miranda.

"I'm Miranda, one of Katelyn's old friends." Miranda smiled at Katelyn.

"Yes, she's one of my old friends."

"Nice to meet you, Miranda."

"It's nice to meet you as well, Mr. and Mrs. Holcomb."

"Please, call us Gwen and Tim," Gwen said with a wink.

"Okay."

After Tim had said the blessing they began to eat, and made small talk. Katelyn wasn't sure when or how to bring up what was on her mind, all she knew was she needed to. She finished off her last bite of fries and washed it down with a big gulp of soda, hoping the awkwardness she felt would soon pass.

"I'm not sure where to start," she said. "I've never been in this position before."

Gwen took her hand, and patted it. "It's okay, my dear. How about we start with prayer."

"That would probably be a good idea."

They all followed Trevor's parents' lead and got on their

knees, leaning up against their chairs.

The demons returned to their lair, bickering and hissing. Melti reached his breaking point. "Quiet!" he yelled.

His eyes narrowed, and he stared at the demons in front of him. "Latar's plan can still be carried out. There will come a time when the door will be opened again, and we'll be right there, waiting and ready."

"What about the book?" Ackmen questioned. "It shouldn't stay in that house. Who knows what will happen to it should she find it."

"True." Melti pointed in the direction of the demons that were still quietly bickering. "Take some of them with you. They can help you find it faster. It's located in the house. Don't assume our enemy has left the girl to fend for herself since the departure of the Warriors. Be on guard. Find the book. Bring it back to me."

Ackmen looked over the spirits in front of him. It was a sad bunch to have to pick from. Finally he chose three and commanded them to stand before him. He let out a displeased growl as he watched them trample over one another as they sought to be first in line.

"Follow me."

The sun had just started to set as they landed in front the house. A familiar feeling crept over each of the gruesome figures. They turned around. "Wonderful," Ackmen grumbled through his pointed teeth. "Melti was right – Guardian's. They can't touch us though, come on."

Kanone stepped forward, his broad stature blocked the door. "State your business here."

Ackmen stepped up. "There's something in there that belongs to us. We want it back."

"You may enter to accomplish your quest, but nothing more. Basholi will go with you." Kanone in a flowing motion moved to the side, giving Ackmen and the small demons ample room to pass.

Ackmen flew over the threshold and gave the command to search the living room. He followed the demons inside and came to an abrupt stop, knocking the spirit in front of him forward. "Stop standing around. They can't hurt us. We must find the book. The sooner the better." He snorted his disgust as he glared over his shoulder at the huge Guardian that trailed their every move.

"Hurry," a small, dark green demon hissed. "I'm feeling weaker by the second." He winced as the spoken prayers sliced through him and out the roof.

"I hate it when God-fearing people are on their knees in prayer. It makes me weaker," Ackmen complained, expelling a nauseous yellow smoke from his mouth.

"Over here, I've found it." The demon picked up the book and then flew out the door, followed by Ackmen and the others.

Kanone greeted Basholi as he retook his stance next to his charge, Miranda. Together they all spread out their wings and covered the five humans beneath them.

Kanone felt Katelyn's uneasiness. He wondered if it had something to do with Miranda being there, or if it was about last night. He tuned his ear to her prayers.

"She knew something was here," he said to his fellow

Guardians. "She could feel it."

Kanone waved them closer, forming a tighter circle of protection around the humans. "That's why she's getting restless. The Commander has given the order to reveal ourselves to her. She needs to know that He didn't leave her alone after the Warriors left."

They nodded their heads in agreement. One by one they removed the shield that hid their glorious light from any mortal's sight. "Katelyn," Kanone spoke gently.

The clear liquid that filled the inside corners of Katelyn's eyes spoke of her relief. Yet there was still a questioning gaze upon her face.

"I'm Kanone, your Guardian. Ask your question. I'll answer it."

"Is something here? Things just don't feel right. I don't feel right."

"Yes, there was something here. They were on a mission, but they are gone now. You don't need to fear."

"A mission?"

"Ackmen was sent to recover a certain object." Kanone watched as her eyes darted back and forth, processing the different thoughts that ran through her mind.

"The book, the one Ackmen," the disgust in her voice came through loud and clear, "the one he threw onto the hood of my car. That's what he was looking for, wasn't it?"

"Yes. We must conceal ourselves now, the others will be finished praying soon. Know that we are still here."

"Always?" Katelyn asked, unsure.

"Always," Kanone replied.

Katelyn followed suit and ended their prayer time with a soft amen. Trevor sat next to her and held her hand. "How are you feeling? Any better?"

"Yes, I am." For the first time in many years a real smile sat upon her lips. A spark had been ignited and she was determined to do whatever possible to keep it burning.

DISCUSSION QUESTIONS

1. Have you ever envisioned a spiritual battle going on around you? For you? How does this idea change your perspective?

2. Have you ever found yourself in a situation where your only option was to call out to God and pray? What happened when you gave it all to God?

3. Have there been times in your life when you've questioned your worth? Why?

4. Have you ever felt like you've done too many things wrong to be accepted by God?

Can I tell you something?
YOU are worth something to God. YOU are worth something to Jesus. God loves you so much that He sent His Son to die for YOU
Jesus loves you so much that He chose to die for YOU!
How does that make you feel?

John 3:16 For God so loved the world that He gave His only begotten Son....

For we wrestle not against flesh and blood,
but against principalities, against powers, against the rulers
of the darkness of this world, against spiritual wickedness in
high places.

Ephesians 6:12 (KJV)

ACKNOWLEDGMENTS

A sincere thank you to the following:
My Lord and Savior, Jesus Christ. Without Him this book
would not have been written.
My family – Thank you for all your support and
encouragement.

Special thanks to:
TreasureLine Publishing
My editors
and
My Readers – May your faith and trust in Him grow more
each day.

About the Author

Kelly Hagen is a wife and mother of three. She's also the author of the children's book *Jake and Jesus*, as well as the mystery romance books *Haunted by the Past,* and *Trent: Everyone has a Past.*

She would love to hear from you at her website, www.kellyhagen.weebly.com and on Facebook at www.facebook.com/AuthorKellyHagen